May and June

By the same author

THE HONG KONG FOREIGN CORRESPONDENTS CLUB

ANTHONY SPAETH

May and June

Secker & Warburg
London

First published in England 1992 by
Martin Secker & Warburg Limited
Michelin House, 81 Fulham Road, London SW3 6RB

Copyright © 1992 by Anthony Spaeth

A CIP catalogue record for this book
is available from the British Library
ISBN 0 436 47654 1

The quote from the Yajur Veda is taken
from 'Prayers, Praises and Psalms,'
translated by V. Raghavan,
G.A. Natesan and Co., Madras, 1938

Set in 11 point Sabon
Printed in Great Britain by
Bookcraft Ltd, Nr. Bath, Avon

For my family

That eyelike sun, may we be seeing it for a hundred
autumns,
May we live a hundred autumns,
May we delight and rejoice for a hundred autumns,
May we be in our places for a hundred autumns,
May we be hearing and speaking for a hundred autumns,
May we be unvanquished for a hundred autumns.
May we be able to see this sun for a long time.

—the Yajur Veda

Christmas

The McNellis house stood on its own on an elevated, trapezoidal plot at the end of town. It was bordered by three roads and, beyond the aging backyard fence, a thruway leading far to the east and far to the west. The house twisted on its small hill, as if from the town and the houses leading there. And with its formidable face of stone, it looked like a country house mistakenly plopped down in the suburbs. Inevitably, the house's aloof reputation transferred to the McNellises themselves, although they hadn't built it and, when the children were young, had frequently considered moving to an ordinary shingled house far from the rumbling thruway. But the kids grew, the impulse to move died, and the house became the McNellises and vice versa. Or, shall we say, it became June McNellis. It was handsome as she was, as all the McNellises were. It was grand, in an easy way. It twisted slightly from town.

Vera Sherman's house was the last in the row that led from town. She considered herself the McNellises' only neighbor and she alone had a substantial view, from her kitchen window, of their house. It was a three-quarters view including the stone face and the converted greenhouse at the east side. She could see every room in the house but one: June and Don's bedroom at the rear. But at night, the lights from that room threw ragged, overlapping rectangles of yellow on the trees beyond. So after sunset, Vera could follow movements through the entire McNellis house.

To Vera Sherman, the McNellis house was as familiar, and as dear, as its occupants. She remembered when it was filled with babies, with teens, with rowdy college kids. She knew long-dead patterns of its lighted windows: when Don had gone away on business, for example, or when the kids were in charge, the stereo blaring, strange cars parked askew on the summer lawn. She recalled crises of the past — Marilyn Beth's birth night being the most dramatic — and she needed but the briefest glance to discern anything out of synch on the McNellis hill.

Vera knew the daily visits of June's two daughters and the excited, odd patterns when Simon returned home from abroad. She had witnessed the alterations ushered in by June's widowhood and wondered if her own house had similarly changed after her husband died. If it had, no one would have observed. For June McNellis, Vera knew, didn't peer out her kitchen window, through the greenhouse, down her hill. She was a valuable friend, an exquisite friend, but June McNellis didn't waste time watching anyone else's life unfold. She was a McNellis and her existence was enough for her. Her family was enough.

And now, the lights signaled that June was waiting in the greenhouse. Vera saw the flickers of the television on the bare, darkened trees. She watched every few minutes, expecting June to move into the dining-room, for June hated the greenhouse, Don's greenhouse, and rarely deigned to sit beneath its ferns. But tonight she remained. All the usual patterns were changing or, more precisely, dying. Vera had watched the girls leave at dinnertime, hurrying to their cars in pained silence. Simon's plane from abroad was late — an unforeseen twist. How he had been awaited! No one expected him to have to enter the house alone.

4

A long, strange car pulled up the McNellis driveway. It sat there for a minute, puffing smoke out its exhaust pipe. A door swung open and a young man emerged, boyishly thin, hauling a small suitcase. He pulled the lapels of his overcoat together and twisted his head toward the garage. He smoothed his hair.

Vera knew: *he's looking for the girls' cars.*

Simon trudged up the steps to the red door with the Christmas wreath. He pushed it open with a quick maneuver of his foot, then closed it gently behind him. Vera held her breath: she imagined him clearing his throat, calling, depositing his suitcase in the den and walking through to the greenhouse. Where he would find his mother, beneath her ferns, alone and dying. Not just that: not just a mother dying. June McNellis dying. The whole town had the same reaction. Death comes to all, of course, and even to June McNellis. Many would have liked to see the spectacle for themselves. None ever would – Vera would see to that. Her mind went back thirty years to the first days in her house, her timorous peeks through that same kitchen window for a glimpse of the talked-about neighbor. *A fashion model*, she had marveled. *What could a fashion model be like as a neighbor?* And her first sighting: June walking to her red convertible, her hair already salt-and-pepper, scolding Holly and carrying Simon in her arms. Vera remembered that day so clearly. And her strange elation over June's beauty.

In the greenhouse, June would have heard Simon's car. Would she try to stand? Or would she arrange herself as best she could, smile up from Don's ugly old recliner and wait for Simon's kiss? When he bent over that yellowed, bony forehead, what would Simon think? Had the girls been able to wash June's hair?

Every family had to go through it, Vera knew, and go through it alone. She fought the impulse to call. For the girls, it seemed easier. They bore it from the first day.

5

Poor Simon had to receive the news by echoing long-distance line. He had to wait, all the time imagining, or not imagining. He had to board that plane alone, travel halfway around the world. To walk through his own front door and attend his mother's death.

She picked up the phone. When she heard Holly's voice, she said simply: 'He's home.'

She took a fresh peek out the window.

'They're in the greenhouse. Simon's probably . . . yes, in the kitchen with his beer.' She laughed her light, unobtrusive laugh. 'I'll let you off so *you* can call. And Holly: does he know Coughlin's new estimate?' She listened. 'And dear – did you manage to wash her hair?'

The greenhouse light burned for another hour and then died suddenly. The light upstairs in Simon's room came on and went out. But the stone house on the hill was never fully darkened these nights. A dim glow shone through the downstairs windows. The rectangle of beeches at the far side remained illuminated all night, disappearing only at dawn. For June McNellis was keeping her bedroom light burning day in and day out during her final days. Along with her radio, according to the girls. It was another new pattern for Vera, the sentinel at the bottom of the hill: the lights burning strong and tirelessly, the radio bellowing life as the former fashion model relinquished it.

'So did she shock you?'

Holly McNellis grasped her coffee mug with calm, freckled hands. Behind her, through the greenhouse, the beeches were expectantly still in the weak morning light.

'I tried to prepare you, Simon. But how could I?'

Holly was the eldest of the three McNellis children, the most conventionally settled and the gentlest. She had inherited her share of the McNellis looks: a round face with wide, serene eyes fringed by blonde curls. But Simon discerned something new in his older sister. Her smile was no longer quite so shy. She tried to dominate the kitchen. She managed to fix Simon with a look, which she had never been able to do before. It said: 'Let's begin. We know where this will end, but not when and not how.' Simon wondered if she was pregnant again. Then he knew that Holly's attitude was born of his mother's approaching death. It signaled her desire to step into June McNellis's place, starting with her house. And maybe ending there. Simon accepted her look and engaged her. Holly faltered, blinking. She smiled at her brother with shy defeat.

Simon was frying Jones sausages, his traditional first day's breakfast at home. His mother had stocked the refrigerator in the past; this time it would have been Holly. He had awakened before dawn with jetlag, wrapped himself in his plaid bathrobe from high school and descended through the chilly house to find his usual favorites in the refrigerator: chilled Clamato, paper packets of sliced salami, a foil-wrapped ham for sandwiches. He had sipped coffee in the greenhouse and watched the dawn develop beyond the backyard fence. In the past, the house had been completely silent in the mornings, except for the rumble of the thruway and the sudden, shocking starts of the aging house. But no longer. The house droned day and night with the sound of his mother's radio. Simon had looked in as he descended, tying the scratchy bathrobe. He saw an unmoving mound covered by a down comforter. Stiff, yellowed hair protruded onto the pillow.

His mother shifted.

'Don't you want me to turn off that light?'

She coughed an affirmation.

'The radio?'

'No, honey.' The voice was raw but purposefully gentle. 'Just the light. Thank you.'

He left her illuminated by blue digits of a clock-radio. Instinctively, he started to shut the bedroom door. But what was the new routine? How did she call if she needed help? He looked once more at the thin, blue mound on the bed and left the door open.

He turned the sausages and began to reply to Holly's question. The phone rang.

'Yesterday was pretty good.' Holly spoke in a bright tone. 'Simon got in . . . yes, the plane was late.' She went on to describe at length the effect of her mother's chemo-therapy treatments.

'Who on earth was that?'

'Harriet.'

'Harriet? Harriet Bauer? Where is she these days?'

'They moved to Phoenix. Mom must have told you. Years ago.'

'Is what's-his-name still alive?'

'Apparently.'

8

'Why do you tell her so much detail?'

Holly, grasping her mug, gave an indulgent smile. 'You'll see. The phone never stops ringing. Harriet Bauer. Mimi Spellman. Winston Rubenoff.'

'Winston *Rubenoff*?'

'You won't believe who you'll talk to in the next few weeks. Especially with Christmas.'

'But all this talk about medication . . . '

'There's nothing else you can say. You get technical. And you repeat yourself over and over again. "The doctors don't know . . . the medication isn't working . . . " What else can you say to these people? That she looks like shit?'

'That must be the first thing they wonder. About Mom.'

'No, they're very positive and, I don't know, very chatty. Easy. Except for Mario.'

'Daddy's tennis friend?'

'He calls every so often. And he just sighs. It's unbelievable. Remember when Daddy died? The same sighs. At the wake, he'll cry in the corner.'

'And his wife will do the talking. I don't think she knows how to sigh. The Jack Spratts of death.' Simon sighed himself. 'Let's not even talk about wakes.'

The morning passed in rapid confusion. The phone rang continually. Twice Simon and Holly went through the living-room, down the hallway, past the den to the darkened bedroom. They stopped speaking halfway. In the bedroom doorway, shoulders touching, they stood looking. The radio blared a phone-in program. June shifted onto her side and adjusted the pillow with clumsiness. A languid hand moved to her forehead. She peered at them and said she'd stay in bed. At noon, Holly left to collect the boys at school. Simon enjoyed the feeling of being alone in the house, or almost alone, but then the phone rang. It was one of his mother's Florida cousins. Simon stumbled through the conversation and found his hands shaking afterwards.

9

Holly's two boys raced through the living- and dining-rooms, shouting hellos. They settled in front of the green-house television. Holly followed with groceries. She started scooping peanut butter. 'Coughlin came the other day. When was it? God, it was just yesterday.'

'What did he say?'

'He said it wasn't a "good situation." '

'So she's not going to make it to June.' Simon shook his head. 'That seemed so cruel. Of all months: June.'

Holly shook her head. 'He didn't say how long, but no. No June.'

The front door slammed. Holly looked at the clock on the stove.

'Marilyn Beth. She's been coming over every day. For lunch – sometimes dinner too.'

'Amazing.' Simon left the kitchen and met his younger sister in the middle of the living-room. They hugged carefully and brushed the tips of their lips. 'I missed you last night, Bethy.'

'You must have been piss-scared to walk in that door. *I* would have been.'

Marilyn Beth was stylishly dressed, as usual: a bright red business suit with a heavy gold chain and a long coat of ivory-colored wool. She had gained weight and was conscious of it. Her gaze flickered nervously from Simon's and her arms, clamped with chunky jewelry, chopped the air. Her hair was unchanged: sandy-colored, extraordinarily thick, worn in a long, bushy ponytail.

'For you.' Marilyn Beth dangled a paper bag with a grease stain. 'Mom made a big fucking deal about it.'

'A Jerry's sandwich. The only thing I miss from home.'

'Thanks a lot,' called Holly.

'The only Italian thing. I hear we're celebrating at the Inn on Friday.'

'It's the first time we've celebrated my birthday since I was ten.' Marilyn Beth pulled a duo of napkin-wrapped hot dogs from a second bag. 'Daddy took us bowling and then made one of his unannounced stops on the way home. To buy the tree. It took hours. My friends had to wait in the car. The *worst* birthday in the world.'

'It's a great birthday, Bethy. We just take a few Christmas presents and give them to you early.'

'Exactly,' frowned Marilyn Beth. 'When I was little, I could see the hole in my pile under the tree. One big present. Three small ones. I always had fewer things in my stocking than you guys.'

'Bullshit, Marilyn.' Holly's hand flew to her mouth. 'Don't listen, boys.'

The two children looked up quizzically from the television set. The smallest, named Paul, said, 'I'm hungry, Mom. What's for lunch, Mom?' He looked back at the television. 'Mom, Jeremy pressed reset. It was my turn! Mom!'

Simon asked Marilyn Beth about work.

'Awful. We just sit waiting for the phone to ring.'

'Wintertime slump!' Holly said brightly. She delivered sandwiches to the boys.

'The summer's no better. I'm getting real tired of mailing lists real fast.'

Holly gave Simon a worried glance. 'It's good money, Marilyn!'

'Tell that to Mr Visa.'

An enormous thump sounded from the dining-room, the most violent sound Simon had ever heard in the house. His head swiveled. Holly ran from the kitchen. The thump sounded a second time. He saw the gilded mirror on the far dining-room wall quiver.

'What the fuck is it?'

At her customary place at the round McNellis dining table, Marilyn Beth doubled over with laughter.

'You should have seen your face, Simon. I've never seen you so scared. Old Mr Cool. It's just *Mom*.'

'I thought the house had ghosts. Ectoplasm.'

'It's her call. She uses the crutch.' Marilyn Beth mimed a vigorous forehand. 'She knocks it above her bed. We can hear it. There.' She pointed at the far wall.

Holly returned. 'She wants some water. And she'll try some Saltines.'

When Marilyn Beth prepared to return to work, Simon asked, 'Aren't there some things we have to discuss?'

'May's visit,' said Holly. 'We have to ask Mom about that. She's driving everyone crazy. Adrian says . . . '

'Fuck May.' Marilyn Beth restored her pink makeup in the gilded mirror. 'And fuck Adrian too. Why does May have to horn in on our Christmas? I'm concerned about the medication. And Mom's eating.'

'I was thinking of the house,' said Simon somberly. 'Don't we have to decide what to do with the house?'

'You two take the house. Just give me my share. In *dinero*.' Marilyn Beth flashed an artificial, beaming smile. 'And Grandma's ring, of course.' Simon looked at her. She dodged his glance.

After she left, Simon queried Holly.

'It's the old plan. Return to Mexico.'

'Oh God. I thought she had given that up years ago.'

'She did give it up, after Daddy actually encouraged her. But when Mom got sick, it began all over again.'

'Is that meathead still in Cancun?'

Holly shook her head. 'It's different this time, completely different. Kevin agrees. She's had a tough time with the illness. Did you notice the extra weight?'

Simon grabbed his midriff.

'I think, and Kevin thinks, her way of reacting to Mom's illness is to go away. To vamoose.' Holly transformed into a doctor with upsetting news. 'And if you don't mind my saying it, I think she's imitating you.'

'My job is abroad . . . '

Holly nodded ambiguously: the doctor who has heard it all.

'What does Mom say?'

Holly looked to the greenhouse to see if the boys were listening. Paul's mouth sagged open and his half-eaten sandwich dipped and rose with his interest in the video game.

'She's steamed.' She pointed to June's place at the dining-room table. 'She sat there and said, "At least it's not another *fucking* motorcycle." '

Simon raised his eyebrows.

'Mom's not mincing words anymore, Simon. And she's kind of, oh, I don't know, giving up. Certain things just don't trouble her anymore. Even Marilyn.'

Simon gestured through the greenhouse. 'The garden's in worse shape than I've ever seen.'

'*That* still annoys her. You know what she said to the gardener? She said, "Just because I have cancer doesn't mean I can't see out my back window." The guy nearly had a heart attack.'

'Poor man,' said Simon. 'Maybe I should bring a gardener from India.'

Simon napped. When he awoke the winter day had faded into an iron dusk. The shadows in the living- and dining-rooms gave the house a ghostly, abandoned look. He walked through the living-room and switched on the kitchen lights and the radio. He turned the dial to a serene jazz station. Simon had never interfered with his mother's radio settings before. He realized it was his kitchen now. June McNellis might never again enter it. She was losing command, as hard as it was to believe, of her kitchen, her house, her beloved garden, the settings on the kitchen radio. And her children. Which was the hardest to believe of all.

There was a bump and Simon dismissed it as a house noise. He heard it again and walked to the kitchen doorway. June was making her way through the blackened living-room. Something was wrong with her silhouette. Then Simon recognized the cane. He moved forward.

June spotted him in the doorway and stopped. She shifted her balance. She bestowed upon him a deliberate smile.

'Hi, honey.' Then she lifted a hand to caution patience. She returned her concentration to walking.

'Let me turn on the lights, Mom. Hold on a second.'

He flicked a switch behind the door. Two floor lamps flashed on, creating, for an instant, a portrait of the dying woman in her living-room. For it was June McNellis's room, as the greenhouse and den had been Don's. The rounded arch of the dining-room helped the effect, along with June's determined decor: the colonial table on the side wall with its swan-necked, crystal candlesticks. On the front wall, between the windows, the full-length painting of June captured at some rare convergence of youth, beauty and class. Visitors commented on the renowned profile, stretched upward to the ceiling. But the true story of the painting was deeper. It showed a woman without doubts. In the years since the picture had been painted, June McNellis had lost her youth, a portion of her country-club class, much of her beauty. But she had remained without doubts. For that reason, the McNellis family appreciated the painting, seeing in it something essential about them and the woman who pulled them all together.

June posed for Simon. The image was a complex one: a dying woman with a steel cane standing unashamed before the painting that potentially mocked her, as it had mocked her plump, menopausal period. The illness had melted away those pounds and June's resemblance to the portrait had briefly reappeared. Her short, signature hair-style was unchanged, except for the white. Gone were the chiffons, of course, but not the sense of style. She wore

14

slacks, a mannish blouse and a long navy-blue cardigan with two leather buttons buttoned at the bottom. The sleeves were rolled twice. June gave a rakish thrust of the rubber-tipped cane. She tipped her chin to the ceiling, making her own mockery of the portrait. The picture had always been too beautiful, too nostalgic, and a little too pink – the only waver of taste in the June McNellis house. But tonight, in the shadows of her living-room, June gave the painting the reality it had always lacked. She gave it its future, its final dignity. In return, the painting provided the expiring woman with a background of innocent color, streaked by the shadows of an iron evening. It fixed in its distant place June McNellis's pastel past.

June smiled to acknowledge the end of the session then started walking with concentration. She walked well, as if recovering from a foot injury. Simon circled the living-room to turn on the other lamps.

'Get the curtains too, honey.' She cleared her throat. 'Those back drapes.'

She settled in her time-honored place at the round dining-room table, the seat closest to the kitchen. Until his death, Don had sat across from her at twelve o'clock, with his back to the windows and the yard. The children had their assigned places. June's chair had always dominated those downstairs rooms, the center of the house. That chair was now missing, stored away for the rest of her days and replaced by a wheelchair with enormous black plastic wheels.

'Coke?'

June nodded. 'And Saltines, honey. They're right on the counter.'

'Have something different, Mom. Something tasty. What about a dill pickle?'

'The Saltines help the nausea.' June looked toward the back window, as if searching for former pleasures. 'A dill pickle does sound good. Yes, that's a good idea. Just one, honey. And don't forget these drapes.'

Simon gave her a glass of Coke. She drank through flaking lips, gasping when the glass was half-emptied.

'Where'd you get the sweater?'

'We found it in Don's closet. No one knows whose it is. I thought it must be Adrian's but he said no.'

'It suits you.'

'Thank you. It's warm. What did you have for lunch?'

Simon held his palms to the ceiling. June nodded with satisfaction. 'You never know with Marilyn. Holly stocked the fridge? And changed the sheets?'

Simon sat at his place and they faced each other at the precise angle that was theirs alone.

'You know Kevin wants this table. Of course, he hasn't *said* anything.'

'They love colonial furniture, those two. Holly would eat oak. She'd make Kevin eat oak.'

'She prefers pine, actually. I always did too. Are you still interested?'

Simon shook his head. 'If they take the house, I think they should have this table. It's perfect here. What's the story with them and the house, Mom? After all.'

'God only knows with those two.' June looked with agitation at her watch. 'Honey, you have to get me my pills. It's past time.'

In the kitchen, Simon rooted among an army of orange plastic vials. 'They're all laxatives.'

'They don't work,' June called. 'Believe me.'

He found the proper pills and delivered them with a renewed glass of Coke. The front door burst open and Holly bustled into the living-room.

'Mom, I forgot. Barbara's coming over tonight. At six-thirty. We told her Saturday she could.'

'Oh God,' said June. 'I don't think I can handle Barbara tonight.'

'It's too late,' Holly said. 'She'll be on her way.'

'I must have felt better on Saturday.'

Simon walked to the front windows. 'Does Barbara have a BMW now? What happened to those dented Rabbits?'

'Guys, I'll try,' said June. 'But if I have to, I'll go in.'

'What about a drink, Mom?'

June grimaced and waved a bony hand.

'What about wine? I'm sure you could get some wine down.'

She hesitated.

'Holly, pour Mom some of that wine in the refrigerator. On the door. It must be Adrian's.'

June straightened herself in the wheelchair. She smoothed her hair with both hands, including the back of the head. The yellowed hair sprung back into disorder. June smoothed it again with uncharacteristically patient hands.

Simon walked to the front door, opened it and looked down the McNellis hill. Barbara approached the house, taking the inclined walk slowly, her arms extended for balance. She wore a black turtleneck sweater and chocolate slacks. Simon realized he had never seen her in a proper overcoat.

When Simon hollered, his breath steamed in the winter evening. 'Bar-ba-*ra*!'

The woman with the black, mannish hair stopped in her tracks. She raised her hands in a *paisano* gesture. 'Si-*mon*! Look at this walk: when your father died, I thought someone might start shovelling it. I mean, who am I? Edmund Hillary?'

'Where's your sherpa?'

She paused, adjusted her legs for balance and bent at the waist. Barbara's laugh was a massive roar. 'My *sherpa*?' Her laugh grated through the air.

'And,' Simon called, 'he loves you.'

A sharp cry came from the doubled-over woman. She raised her hand in a mute plea, gave another bellow and continued walking steadily. When she reached the doorway, she enveloped Simon in a muscular embrace.

'A *sherpa*. My God! You know I can't even stand cats.'

'And they clean themselves.'

She shook with laughter.

'And hardly drink. Well, they drink milk.'

Barbara's face was creased with laughter and there were tears in her eyes. She patted him on the top of his head. She said in a stage whisper, 'How is she? Is she still vomiting? Is it driving you crazy or what?'

'*Hello* . . . ' The ragged voice abruptly died. A cough followed. Then, with vibrance, 'Hello Barbara.'

Simon and Barbara looked from the doorway. June was standing at her wheelchair, the steel cane extended with ironic rakishness.

'My God, she looks just like Doc with that cane. And that wheelchair! What are you doing with a wheelchair, June McNellis? You look just like your father. I don't know about you but I'm not getting in any wheelchair.'

'Yes Barbara, I know that.' June turned gingerly and maneuvered herself back into the wheelchair.

'I'm not ready to die.' Barbara went to the back of the wheelchair, bent over and kissed June on the forehead.

'Nobody's ready to die, Barbara.'

Barbara pulled June's head to her bosom. The two children made eye contact. Holly smiled acceptingly and Simon turned away. When he returned his gaze, Barbara was looking at the ceiling and blinking.

'You look terrible – no, you've looked *better*, but you don't look terrible. You look . . . like *Doc*. What can I say?'

Simon looked for embarrassment on his mother's face or, at the least, an expression of wry resignation. But it wasn't there. She smiled at Simon as if she pitied him.

'Dad was a hundred and two, Barbara.' June adjusted herself in the wheelchair. A grimace of pain flashed on her face.

'He didn't look a day over ninety-five,' Barbara said.

'And neither do you, Mom,' said Simon. Everyone laughed. 'I'm sure that's Doc's sweater.'

'That might explain this stain.' June scratched at the thick sleeve with a fingernail.

'You're not bald,' said Barbara. 'So you don't look exactly like Doc. That's something.'

June smoothed her chemo-thinned hair. 'They tried.'

'A drink, Barbara?'

'Nothing, dear,' said Barbara. 'Or maybe a beer. What are you drinking, June?'

'Wine.'

Barbara gaped. 'I've never seen you drink a glass of wine in my life. You're becoming an Italian.'

'She's become an Italian,' Simon said. 'And it's killing her.'

'I can't swallow beer anymore. My throat.' June reached into the sweater pocket and removed a packet of Carlton 100s.

'Sweet Jesus,' Barbara cried. 'What on earth do you think you're doing, June McNellis?'

June gave a small, embarrassed grin. She lit the cigarette and inhaled deeply.

'After all this – all you've gone through?'

'Holly refuses to buy them for me,' June said. 'Marilyn Beth will.'

'I just can't believe it.'

Simon went to his mother's side. 'Barbara, what's it going to do? Give her cancer?'

'Still. Jesus Christ . . . '

'And they are low-tar.'

Barbara started to laugh. She put her face in her hands.

When she looked up, her mouth open to speak, a startled look took her. 'Vera. I didn't hear you come in.'

Vera Sherman stood at the dining-room arch holding a large, foil-covered plate. She wore neutral-colored slacks, white sneakers and a pink sweater. There was a gentle twinkle in her eyes, glad as always to be part of a McNellis gathering. Her ginger hair was dusted with snowflakes.

'I saw Barbara's car.' She handed Holly the plate. 'I thought you might want some cake. Hello Simon. I'm glad you're home at last.'

Simon kissed her.

'Hello Vera.'

'How's it going, June?'

'I'm drinking white wine. So it can't be that bad.'

'I guess not.'

'And puffing cigarettes,' Barbara added. 'If I hadn't seen it . . . '

'Oh well,' said Vera, looking quickly at Holly and Simon. She giggled. 'I hear you're celebrating Marilyn Beth's birthday at the Inn.'

'Marilyn says Mrs Sherman is the only person who remembers her birthday,' said Holly.

'I couldn't forget Marilyn Beth's birthday. I remember that night as if it was yesterday. Ross woke me up and said, "Look. All the lights are on. It's the baby!" He called the hospital to alert them. He threatened to fire them all if anything went wrong. I'll never forget the house: it was lit up like a Christmas tree!'

'Hey, what's happening with this house?' asked Barbara. 'Have you made any decisions? Take my advice: list it fast. The market is terrible.'

'*I'm* hoping Holly and Kevin take it,' said Vera.

June smiled and looked at Holly.

'You should take it,' said Barbara. 'It's a great house. In great condition. I'll give you that, June.'

'I don't think I could get used to new neighbors after thirty years,' said Vera.

'We don't know if we can afford it.' Holly looked distressed for the first time that day. 'And Kevin has some problems, I think, with the idea.'

'That's garbage,' said Barbara. 'It's your mother's house. What problems?'

June chuckled and tapped her cigarette on the ashtray.

'Isn't the market falling?' asked Simon. 'I mean, how much is it worth?'

'We'd have to find a buyer for *our* house,' insisted Holly.

The phone rang and Holly escaped the conversation to answer it. At the same time, the front door pushed open and Marilyn Beth entered. Barbara rose and gave her a bear-hug. 'So no one remembers your birthday, godchild?'

'The worst birthday in the world,' said Marilyn Beth, removing her coat. 'Mrs Sherman's the *only* one who remembers.'

'Vera! You don't have a drink.'

'Nothing, June. Maybe just an iced tea.'

'Sorry,' said Simon. 'We don't have any. It seems Mom used to keep the iced-tea supply going.'

'They thought fairies did it,' June said. 'Have a glass of wine.'

'Oh no,' Vera giggled.

'Fairies must have also filled up the salt-shaker on the stove,' said Marilyn Beth, taking her chair. 'I'd never seen it empty until last week. I didn't even know where the salt was.'

'See Mom,' said Simon. 'We *are* going to miss you. Iced tea, salt, turning our socks right side out after washing.'

'Fairies,' said June, lowering her gaze to the ashtray. She lit another cigarette with faltering fingers.

June, Simon and Marilyn Beth were all in their set places; Vera sat in Holly's chair and Barbara had taken

Don's former place in front of the windows. Holly finished the phone call in the kitchen but immediately the phone rang again.

'How's the job, godchild?' asked Barbara.

'Great,' said Marilyn, 'if you like looking at mailing lists all day long.'

'What do you do with those mailing lists, Marilyn?' asked Vera. 'You must do a lot. I get more catalogues each day.'

'Well, you get a list. You have a customer who wants to sell to men. This happened today. Mail-order tools. So you go through your list, change all the "Mrs" to "Mr" and sell that list to the tool company.'

June had a brief coughing fit, waved away concern, and said in a raspy voice, 'What if he's dead? What if Mr Smith happens to be dead, Marilyn? I've gotten catalogues from those goddamned lists long after your father was gone. And it annoyed me to no end.'

'Me too,' said Vera.

A lively discussion arose about catalogues, junk mail, unsolicited credit cards. Holly put down the phone and rejoined the group.

'That was Coughlin. He's sending a new painkiller in the morning. But if this doesn't work, we'll have to go onto the steroids.'

'Steroids!' exclaimed Barbara.

'You'll have to give back your medals, Mom,' said Simon.

Barbara pushed back her chair to hold the table edge. 'Her medals!' she gasped. 'I want to be here for the first injection. June McNellis taking steroids. At Christian Court, we couldn't even get her into the pool.'

'I never saw any of the nuns in the pool,' June said, picking at her crimson nail polish. 'They liked those god-damned whistles, though.'

'The other call was from Adrian, Mom. He said he'd

be here Friday, in time for Marilyn's dinner. He'll cut short one of his workshops.'

'He's been coming up often, hasn't he?' said Vera. 'I see these cars in the driveway and then I realize it's Adrian. With a rental.'

'He has a lot of workshops in this area.' June brushed the flaked nail polish from her lap. 'It *is* nice. Holly, you or Kevin will get him at the airport?'

'The Inn was one of the first places we went when we moved here,' Vera said. 'It was tiny then.'

'I hope I can get through it. Although I'm feeling pretty good tonight.' June held aloft her wine glass. 'Honey, could you get me another?'

'Maybe the steroids will help you, Mom,' said Simon. 'Perk up your decathlon.'

'Eating at the Inn is a decathlon,' said Holly. 'The prime rib.'

Barbara looked at her watch, put her hands on the table as if to rise and said, 'Where are those medals, June. I'll just bring them over to the committee.' At the same time Marilyn Beth rose and put on her coat.

'You're not staying for dinner?' asked Simon.

'My lessons begin tonight. At Manhattanville.'

'What lessons?' asked Barbara.

'Spanish.'

Simon saw his mother shake her head with disgust.

'Didn't you learn it in high school?' asked Barbara.

'She failed it in high school,' said Holly.

'Bethy,' said Simon. 'Couldn't you have waited?'

'Waited for what?' Barbara, standing, looked puzzled. June stabbed the ashtray with her cigarette. Vera's face had a small smile.

'For me to croak,' June said. 'That's what.'

Barbara's laugh sounded like a siren. She went behind June's chair and grasped her bony shoulders.

'It's just Spanish, Mom,' said Marilyn Beth. 'You make it sound like I'm digging your grave.'

'Anyway, mothers don't croak,' said Holly. 'They "pass on." '

'Like a bad restaurant meal,' said June.

'In Cancun,' said Simon.

'Or New Delhi,' retorted Marilyn Beth.

Barbara's head was thrown back in laughter. June was laughing too, happy at the center of her jousting family.

'Look, if these lessons kill anyone,' said Marilyn, 'it's going to be me. *Es el hombre que tiene las llaves en la mano.*' That's all I can remember after three years.'

'*En el* mano,' corrected Holly.

'You're going back to Mexico?' asked Barbara, wiping tears.

'It's always been a dream of mine.'

'I dreamt of being a rock star,' said Simon. 'But instead of satin pants, what do I end up with?'

'A turban,' replied Marilyn Beth. 'And what are those dirty things they wear between their legs?'

'It's called a byline,' said Simon. 'Oh – you mean Indians.'

'I wanted to be a great painter,' said Holly.

'I never understood this about young people,' said June. 'I never wanted to be anything but what I was. A mother. That was enough for me.'

'I felt the same way,' said Vera.

'I might have felt the same way, Mom, if my father had been a millionaire.'

'Oh Marilyn. That's not the point at all. It has nothing to do with money.'

Marilyn Beth departed and Barbara prepared to follow. 'Okay kiddos,' she said. 'Back to the gold mines. No nuns in the pool – I'll remember that.'

'Those goddamned whistles,' said June. 'They expected us to obey them like slaves.'

'What was that nun's name, June?'
' "Go Take A Shit For Yourself?" '
Somehow Vera had never heard the famous tale. 'I have to sit down for this,' said Barbara. 'I wish you had the yearbook, June. What do you mean you don't have your Christian Court yearbook?' With alternating narrations, the two matrons delivered their classic routine for the last time. Everyone laughed until tears showed. Barbara was still laughing when Simon and Holly walked her to the door.

'My God, she looks awful. I can't believe it, Holly, Simon. I never thought I'd see such a thing. She was so beautiful. I mean just look at that painting. Lord, what are you doing to us? Keep me informed, kids. I've known your mother longer than anyone else in my life. I don't have to come over. Just let me know how it's going. Promise? I won't bother her. Or you. Just call. Your mother's my oldest friend.'

Vera unobtrusively left, squeezing Simon's arm at the door. When June announced her intention to retire, Holly said, 'Mom, we have to decide about May. Adrian says she's driving him crazy.'

'I can't fight her any more. Tell her to come. Thanksgiving was horrible but we'll have to put up with it. But after the weekend.'

'Adrian says she is family, after all.'

June shook her head. 'Not in my book.'

When she had walked slowly from the living-room, Holly said, 'That's her best night in weeks. I think your being here helps. I really do.' They were interrupted by a banging on the wall. Holly did the night's final ministrations. While she was away, Simon poured her a glass of wine.

'I can't tell you how hard it was getting your phone call in Madras. The line – it was so bad.'

Holly looked at him sympathetically. 'I know. We all knew. Mom was so worried for you.'

'What's her attitude about the house? Does she care if it actually gets sold?'

'No,' Holly said thoughtfully. 'I think she did, but not anymore. She hasn't said much. Kevin and I really have to discuss it.' They talked a few minutes about real-estate prices and the difficulty in finding buyers. Simon yawned and blamed jetlag.

'I hear Kevin wants this table.'

'Oh God, did Mom mention that? It's so unimportant. If you want it . . . '

Simon shook his head.

'He's always said he'd love to raise kids around this table. Just like Mom and Daddy. He really idolizes them.' When Holly left, Simon cleared the table, drained her half-emptied wine glass and turned on the radio. A jazz instrumental filled the downstairs. But Simon was unnerved by the black, staring panes of the greenhouse and its still ferns. He retired to his room upstairs. He wandered around it, marveling at its unchanged quality, something he both cherished and despised: the familiar paperbacks, the trinkets, the embalmed, shrunken clothing in the attic closet. He stood in the middle of the room and recognized his weariness. Just as he was dropping off to sleep, a noise startled him. He opened the bedroom door and listened. He called – 'Mom?' – but there was no reply. He returned to bed, wondering about the house noises that were alien to him. Had he forgotten them? Was that possible: like forgetting an old pet, even after it licks your hand? Or were they new voices? Wasn't that more likely: that the past was dead and the voices of the present unfamiliar?

Simon drifted off to the sound of his mother coughing downstairs.

Damned money worries niggled at May, beginning when the morning still had something wonderful to it, a morning of birds and sharp sunshine and folded ten-dollar bills unexpectedly scattered with the newly dried clothes. Surprises were definitely possible: really, really nice mail, valentines, a spate of happy, long-distance phone calls. How could people be so damned cheap about such things? Then the phone actually rang. A long-distance call from a fruity Northerner canceling his Christmas booking to go to Williamsburg instead. May was sweet, of course, and tried utterly hard to be gracious as well, although who could help but ask, 'Didn't they close it, darlin? After that whoppin big fire? When everyone died?' She flipped through the ledger to excise the man and his companion. The pages and pages of blank spaces depressed her. She found their names – written in a bright, optimistic hand with big circles dotting the i's – and she crossed them out slowly and firmly until she actually penetrated the following two weeks. Two equally blank weeks, defaced with a thick pencil line that just wouldn't erase, try as she might. Then Carmen, May's colored girl, chose to arrive, giving her usual sourpuss greeting. Carmen, of course, could teach a crocodile to kill time, although that's not how May described her to the outside world. Carmen was wonderful, May's *best friend*, they giggled like roommates in boardin school, darlin. Whole mornings go by and not a stitch of work gets done – *that* happened to be true – what with the laughin and private jokes and secrets. Yes, secrets! Everybody has secrets. May knew this more than anyone. Perhaps even Carmen had a tiny secret. Although no one would attempt to guess, especially on Monday mornings, dragging her godawful bag. And that hair! Coloreds, in May's opinion, had a long, long way to go.

'Just do all the rooms, Carmen, whether they've been used or not.' May heard a growl which was not, by any stretch of the imagination, attractive. 'And don't forget the Christmas wreaths, Carmen, like Monday.' May stared at the phone and bit her lip. She said, without bothering to look up, 'You don't have all God's good day, dear.'

She heard Carmen's bumps as she worked the back-room. She stopped to think and slurped her instant coffee. She snatched up the phone and punched the number of the nursing home.

'No, don't put her on nurse, I wouldn't want to trouble her or interrupt her morning rituals, just tell me how everythin's goin today. I've been so concerned recently. Oh, I was there last week. Yes I most certainly was. You must not have seen me.' She listened and rolled her eyes. Those eyes. Mama had been so insistent about eye makeup. And she had a point, of course. God gives, but there's nothing wrong with a little artificial emphasis. But sometimes it did look too thick, in photographs at least. Although no woman likes her own photographs. June McNellis had taken to snipping her image out with nail scissors, leaving behind odd, gray cocoons in otherwise happy group shots. May had several such photos: her smilin like mad, her arm around an angular hole in the middle. Which just proved that all is vanity. June McNellis could have made that her motto. The motto of the entire family, perhaps, inscribed on one of those $45 fake coats of arms. 'Oh, maybe you're right, dear, maybe it was the week before, things at the hotel have been *so* busy.' She watched Carmen lug a vacuum up the stairs. 'We're all suites, you know. Has Ruthie dear said anything about her niece? About June? June *McNellis*, from up North? Well I know lots of your patients are from up North. I believe we should start sendin *our* old wrecks to New York and New Jersey and, oh, I don't know, New Hampshire – isn't that an idea? Well, I didn't mean it that way. Ruthie's had no more of those silly tales about plane crashes?' She listened impatiently. 'But wasn't that funny? A plane crash? It was that niece, June McNellis, from up North, who she imagined in that plane crash. Do you remember now or maybe you don't pay any attention to the old dears? I just wonder what she will think up next. I love her like a . . . ' May hesitated. 'Like my own great-aunt, if you know what I mean.'

May dragged on her cigarette, stubbed it out savagely and punched the phone ten times.

'Good mornin, darlin. Is it as *wonderful* a day up there as it is down here? The sun is shinin and we're all ready to pull up our socks and go, oh I don't know, polo-playin or somethin.' May looked about to make sure Carmen was out of earshot. 'Carmen and I, we're just sitting here havin marigold tea and . . . tellin dirty jokes. Like regular sisters, aren't we Carmen darlin?' May laughed and laughed, repeating the joke twice while opening her date book. 'No, I haven't received it yet, Adrian darlin. But I'll look forward to it. You find such interestin things in the newspaper.' She listened. 'Yes, of course. But Adrian, I'm gettin anxious about June. I'm dyin, darlin, to get up there and get my hands dirty just helpin out. The girls are so busy and they have their children, or Holly does. And . . . ' She listened. 'Yes, I know Simon is there, but Adrian darlin, I just got off the phone with poor Ruthie and she's feelin pitifully lonely and I had the most *wonderful* idea!

We can make it a regular party! Ruthie can come with me to June's for Christmas! It's just what her spirits need – she is still goin on and on about June and that plane crash, I can't imagine what put such an idea in her stupid old head – and I'm sure they'd have wheelchairs on Amtrak. I talked to the doctors at the home and they say the chance of her pneumonia coming back is . . . '

May hung up and sat with her cold Nescafé and cigarettes for a long time. Carmen brought in the mail and she ripped open the envelope from Adrian. It contained a newspaper clipping reporting that two out of three restaurant ventures failed. She crumpled it into a ball and shot it into the corner. Her hand snatched the telephone receiver. She punched it ten times, her eyes grew wide and she put the phone down.

'No!' Her voice was choked. She had trouble catching her breath. She vowed not to talk to herself. Carmen might catch her again. She flicked on the television and watched an episode of a soap opera. Then she dialed the number again.

'Hello Simon darlin. How are you this great, wonderful mornin. Why you're right – it's become just a great wonderful *afternoon*! I was thinkin about you so much yesterday, or the day before. I thought: he's gettin on the plane now, he's gettin off, he's gettin on again, God knows where. He's, oh I don't know, he's eatin a plastic omelet or Prawns à la . . . Dupont or somethin.' She gave her girlish laugh. 'How is Mum today?'

His reply surprised her.

'Well, darlin, that's exactly what I was hopin you'd all say. I'm glad Mum is so . . . the twenty-third is what, a Mon . . . Tuesday . . . Excuse me darlin, what did you say?'

May listened with an intent look.

'Why June darlin, your voice is just the greatest thing I've heard in a long time. You sound so, oh, *wonderful*.

Well, yes, and a bit scratchy. But I believe we're all goin to have a wonderful, *wonderful* holiday, with chestnuts and popcorn and the whole family together, and, well. And what? Steroids?' She gave a startled laugh. 'I'm sure I don't know what you mean.' She listened. 'Oh . . . well save some for *me* darlin. I'll join you! Why not? They sound like just the thing I could use about now.'

Simon got back on.

'Simon darlin, I hope you and Mum have the most wonderful, *wonderful* rest of the day!'

She hung up, having totally forgotten about poor neglected Ruthie, June's great-aunt and May's chosen Trojan horse to get into the McNellis house for the holiday. Ruthie, it seemed certain, would celebrate her Christmas with a nursing-home version of Turkey à la Dupont, surrounded by all those shrunken, sour, gray heads wagging with complaint around the scuffed linoleum tables. Maybe May would pay a visit before she left. Although there was little time, what with all the shopping that would be required, Christmas and all. As May's Mama used to say, when you're on a budget, just shop a little harder! Poor Ruthie. It was such a dreary old nursing home. And so ridiculously expensive. The head nurse had refused to divulge Ruthie's balance. May feared her estate would be depleted by the following year. More gleanings might be available at Christmas. People always spoke out on holidays – and during illnesses. Although the McNellises were maddeningly tight-lipped about family finances, Marilyn Beth was a bet. She appreciated money. Although it had to be admitted she was notoriously uninformed and maddeningly incurious.

Carmen slurred her farewell. May revealed that she had been asked North for Christmas, begged almost, and she couldn't turn down her favorite sister-in-law – her only sister-in-law, if the truth was told – who was so ill, and so beautiful, with such a beautiful, *wonderful* family, too bad the husband had died too. But that happened to the best of us. Of course, her own child *would* miss her and May had half-planned to visit Daniel in New Orleans, which would have brightened his spirits and God knows they needed brightening and not always through pharmacology. But this was more important. May wagged her finger at Carmen and adopted a serious look. For this was, of course, something transcendent. Something more important than almost anything else. This was, after all, *cancer*.

'If only we could open up these windows and let in the wonderful fresh air,' May exulted. 'And the light!'

'They're not openin any further,' said Carmen. 'That's why this place is so gloomy.'

'Thank you Carmen.' May pointed with a thin, scarlet fingernail. 'You missed that crumpled-up thingie in the corner.'

Only after Carmen left did May think back to her last, undeniably unsatisfying stay at the McNellises. She had felt less than welcome. The two daughters had tried to exclude her from the medical talk. June herself had started to shut down like a pitiful fire out of wood. And, as always, May was not invited to share in the phone calls to and from Simon, which were even more frequent than usual. June did love her calls to Simon. May's only recourse was to snatch the phone whenever it rang, to claim that triumphant little beep from very, very far away. She recognized the potential perils of the upcoming trip. Simon would actually be there, the visiting royal of the McNellises, skinny Mr Professional in his jeans and crew-neck sweaters. She had never liked the way he looked at her: it was neither polite nor kind. To May's mind, Simon was the McNellises' secret weapon in their war against her inclusion in the family. He was the big gun they pulled out when the rest were too fainthearted: skinny, superior, a touch feminine, with silver plate for a heart and synthetic diamonds for eyes. June's damned eyes. And that wasn't all. Everyone knew that when Simon was home he enjoyed a monopoly of June McNellis's attention. Trying to join a conversation between the mother and son was as gratifying as playing chaperone to Romeo and Juliet.

But May decided to concentrate on the brighter side. She reminded herself of the truly wonderful stuff she had brought home from Thanksgiving: a lambskin rug that no one was using, a dust-covered carafe with just the tiniest chip along the edge, a pair of blue Calvin Klein socks for Randall next door, who would adore Calvin Klein if she could afford him. She had purchased a wonderful calendar at Odd Lots, an assortment of cute clips and paper supplies for the hotel, a starter set of china for poor Daniel, although all of these had to be left behind in June's den closet or May would have broken her shoulder carrying the bags. May had managed only one long *wonderful* talk with June, curtailed by a coughing-cum-vomiting fit which had been undeniably ugly. The next day came the bad news from the cancer doctor, or the latest bad news, and then Adrian's arrival, stirring the pot as it always did. It was only on her last night, when everyone had gone to bed, that May decided on a little late-night bonus. She sipped her coffee and admired the cup. So pretty and such a *wonderful* name: Iceland Poppy. No, the trip had not been very gratifying at all. But, as May's mother always said, life provides its compensations. May steeled herself for a difficult visit at the McNellis house. She knew there weren't many left.

The routine of a sick house is an anti-routine, and the days leading to Christmas became discombobulated for Simon McNellis. By itself, the telephone dissolved patterns, even patterns of hope and despair. 'Mrs Becker, the doctors don't really say. The first chemo wasn't successful, but they'll try again after Christmas. One medication seems to work and then . . . ' Tender sentiments concluded each conversation, disturbing any rational feelings that had begun to form, as skin can't form on milk that ceaselessly boils. And then the telephone rang again, pulling into it, in varied form, the same non-conversation. 'It's a question of balancing the painkiller and the anti-nausea pills, we think. But the doctors can't say, or won't say . . . '

June's good times were widely spaced and unpredictable. Simon would sleep until 8:30, rush downstairs guiltily and find a vacant, foreign living-room, drapes weakly pulled against the new day. At nightfall, he made elaborate dinners – Potatoes Anna, Caesar salads, marinated flank steaks: a succession of June's historical favorites – and she would choose to remain in bed. After hours of preparation, he would eat in ten minutes, kept company by the oozing jazz from the kitchen radio. He'd scowl at the television listings and punch all the buttons, backward and forward, on the cable-television machine. When he read, the black greenhouse windows stared at him; in the

34

living-room, it was the dull, fearful drapes. The house continued to groan as it never had before. His only escape was to the room of his childhood where he could masturbate without adolescent precautions – locked doors, flushed tissues – and then sleep, shutting out the sound of his mother's coughing. But even these comforts were impossible before 10:30 or 11:00, for the downstairs telephone was certain to intrude.

The girls came at unpredictable times. The door would crash open, children's feet would pound across the living-room, Marilyn would call a sardonic greeting. The mail brought messages from June McNellis's relatives and acquaintances, along with preposterous medical bills. Both had to go into the sickroom for June's comment or rejection. Simon lost track of days and dates. His jetlag, an early excuse for disorientation, became a lingering illness. He'd start awake from desolating afternoon naps, scared at the house's sudden silence. From his pillow, he saw winter sky and trembling beeches. Simon gazed at them and was reminded of the distance he had put between himself and his childhood home. The view outside his current bedroom half a world away: a leafy gulmohar in a cobalt sky, once home to its own monkey, or so said the servants. Before that: the shabby rooftops of an avenue of sex, brilliant with neon promise every nightfall. Before that: a tiny rice paddy circumscribed by snowy concrete. An after-nap tear glided down Simon's cheek. The naked beeches waved silently in the invisible wind, as they must have through all his years away from home. Then the telephone would make its indomitable cry. He would rush down the stairs, or dash in from the yard, or push through the red door with stiff brown bags from the supermarket prepared to find a dead mother, hand stretched in vain appeal, diamond ring glinting accusingly. But there was only that darkened room, the small silhouette under the down comforter, the drone of the radio. Simon cursed that last insistent ring, often cut in half. Each missed call seemed a tragedy. The telephone's urgent pretension: all the McNellises had become its slaves.

One afternoon, Simon asked Holly, 'Should we talk with her? I mean, have you felt the need to say goodbye? In some special way?'

Holly's brow wrinkled with concern.

'To clear up old . . . I mean, we've got the time. It seems.'

'What do you want to say?'

Embarrassed, Simon shifted the subject.

On Friday, June's elder brother Adrian arrived in his customary maelstrom of confusion. He changed planes at the last minute, prompting a half-day of phone calls and a minor mixup. When Kevin, Holly's husband, arrived at the local airport, Adrian had been standing outside the terminal for forty minutes, slapping his thigh with a D.C. newspaper. At the McNellis house, he whipped off his Irish hat and announced that he *had* intended to take a nap. But Marilyn Beth's birthday dinner was set for 7:00.

'You eat so damn early in the suburbs. What's *wrong* with a little *nap*, for God's sake.' (It was Adrian's famous ironic tone, employed when he was most earnest.) He looked at his watch and then, peripherally, at Kevin. 'Just thirty minutes.' Adrian's naptime had been wasted at an air terminal thanks to a McNellis conspiracy, not the first, executed by Kevin. When Kevin said he'd fetch Holly, Adrian had trouble meeting his eye.

'She's probably waiting out in the snow,' Adrian said. 'I've got some interesting clippings for you, Simon.'

'Let's go in and see Mom.'

Adrian was a taller, fitter version of June McNellis. The years had pampered him and he drew women still. But there were moments when time's kind curtain fluttered and Adrian's future could be spied.

'Coughlin isn't optimistic I hear.' His voice dropped to

a paranoiac whisper. 'I've never had much *faith* in him, *frankly*.' Adrian straightened up and began to revive. 'Okay.' He clapped his hands. 'Let's go. Have you gained weight, old man? All those curries? I *never* seem to get a decent *nap* around this place.'

They traversed the living-room, looped around the front hallway and headed for the rear of the house. June was unaltered: a narrow lump beneath a cushion of down, the radio blaring a harsh New York accent.

Adrian gave his horrible whisper. 'She's *too much* with that radio.'

'I heard you come in,' said June, shifting. 'Hello Adrian.'

'The medication's still giving you a hard time, June. Can we turn this down?'

'Let me get some lights.' Simon crossed to the white wicker dresser. He craned over the top of a table lamp. The socket was empty, as he remembered it from decades before. At the lamp's base were Asian artifacts, silver heirlooms and family photos: himself as a black-eyed infant, his dead father Don on a boulder in swirling water, his legs scissored open.

'How was the trip?'

'How does this radio . . . okay. I *got* it. The trip was fine but the connections are not what they should be. I had a bit of a squabble with the girl at Continental.' Adrian kissed June's forehead and executed a ginger, extended hug. A foreign arm rose from June's bed – its color from the sea, its texture from a previous century – and she patted his back.

'When does May arrive?'

'Monday afternoon, Mom.'

'Are you up for the big birthday *soirée*?'

'I don't know, Adrian.' She put her hand on her forehead. 'I don't know about anything anymore.'

'Wait and see how you feel,' said Simon. 'We have

time.' He looked at his watch. 'I have to pick Grace up at the station.'

'Grace?'

'My friend from the editorial page.'

June started coughing. 'Simon's old *girlfriend*.'

'She's back in New York now,' Simon explained, 'after a long time in Hong Kong. You met her, Adrian, I'm sure. Mom and Dad used to have dinner with her in Hong Kong. After they visited me. She has those huge glasses.'

'Our yearly shopping stops,' said June.

'Glasses?' Adrian shook his head and stretched, putting a hand on his lower back. 'Frankly, I was hoping for some shuteye, but this dinner reservation is for seven. Why don't we go to Gus's? It's your mother's favorite. We could get a table there at any time. Don't you want some scrod from Gus's, June?'

'It's *Bethy's* birthday,' said Simon.

'I don't want anything,' said June.

In the kitchen, Adrian admitted his sister had deteriorated. He said his hopes were on the new medication.

'What medication?'

'The steroids.'

'Come on, Adrian. That's last-ditch.'

'Marilyn Beth didn't mention that.' Adrian paced the kitchen with a pursed expression. 'Your mother always loved the scrod at Gus's.' He looked at his watch. 'No time for a nap now. We'll have to bring it in some night.'

Grace stood on the station platform, peering through the drizzle from beneath a pale hand. In the car, Simon laughed. It was quintessentially Grace: self-aware, theatrical and just a little bit ludicrous. Shielding her eyes from some unaccountably absent tropical sun. He honked and she craned her head deliberately. She nodded with satisfaction and struggled with a black, man's umbrella. Grace was tall and walked slowly and determinedly, with a slight ungainliness. She had straight brown hair with bangs.

Her clear-rimmed glasses magnified small, impatient eyes. Simon recognized her beige raincoat: he had bought it for her in Hong Kong. When she settled herself in the front seat, Grace extended a smooth, pale cheek for a kiss. Then she sighed.

'I was settled perfectly nicely.' Grace's voice was flutey with a wide range she employed for even the simplest anecdote. 'I had my crossword puzzle *and* my Tab *and* all my things on the seat beside me *just* where I wanted them. Then some Japanese man insisted on the seat.' She sighed again. 'He opened a can of beer and *belched*' – Grace's eyes widened behind her spectacles – 'not *once*, not *twice*, but *three* times.' Her lips parted to reveal small teeth and wide, baby-pink gums. 'And to top it off, we got up to leave at the same station.' She sighed once more and gestured at the passing trees. The suburbs, Grace suggested, required much patience. She reached back to tame her unwieldy umbrella.

On the way back to the house, she related the latest company gossip. Simon described his mother's condition. 'I hope this isn't too uncomfortable for you. A sick dinner in the suburbs.'

She patted his arm. 'I'm honored.' She took off her glasses and rubbed the bridge of her nose. She looked at Simon with narrow, accusing eyes. 'Is there something you ought to tell me? Remember that *horrible* Christmas with my aunt whose jaw was cut away? And Mummy didn't *tell* me? I went up to her, *all* bravery, planning to give her a big *kiss*!' Grace shook her head, restored her spectacles and blinked bravely at the passing landscape. 'I still can't imagine what my expression was like.'

Adrian welcomed Grace warmly, seemingly pleased by her attractiveness. She went straight to the McNellis refrigerator and glared at Simon.

'I'm sorry,' he said. 'I forgot to buy Tab.'

Grace sighed and settled for a Coke. 'What happened to those tiny dogs you used to have?'

'Claire and Joe?'

'The ones with the little teeth.'

'They died.'

'How?'

Simon looked at Grace balefully.

'Oh dear. Dog cancer. I better not mention Claire and Joe to your mother.'

'They hardly smoked,' said Simon.

'Only, uh, after chow,' called Adrian.

'And . . . ' Simon made a humping motion in the air.

'Oh Simon!' Grace shook her head. She moved to the dining-room table and settled next to Adrian. They talked of June and illness. Grace described her father's death of cancer. Adrian said, 'When I was in high school I was a great Bing Crosby fan. One of the biggest. And I remember thinking one day that someday he would *die*. It was the shock of my life.' Adrian started to chuckle. 'I started *crying*. I couldn't *imagine* a world without "Der Bingle." Sime – did you hear that?' When Holly arrived, wearing jewelry and a rare brush of makeup, Simon gave the signal. They went to June's bedroom. Simon returned moments later.

'She says she's feeling pretty good. She'll go!'

June appeared in her red suit with the black trim. It was a favorite outfit from a trimmer time. Holly said, 'Ta da! Nancy Reagan!'

'Not too long ago,' responded June, 'I was looking like Barbara Bush. I'm quite pleased with myself. Hello Grace. It's good to see you. Thank you for the letter.'

Grace put out her cigarette, rose and lumbered to the front hallway. She gave June a somber kiss. June smiled and moved slow hands through her short, white hair.

Holly helped her into her coat.

'I'm sure you're *really* pining for a good piece of scrod,

June,' said Adrian. 'Although the beef *is* pretty good at the Inn. You don't get much of that where you are, Simon.'

'Breaks my caste.'

'I don't know about eating,' said June. 'Give me your arm, Adrian, would you? Holly – the cane?'

At the Inn, Marilyn Beth was waiting with a wide-brimmed Margarita before her. She wore a new black leather jacket. There were jokes about age. Marilyn Beth told Grace, 'The *worst* birthday in the world.' Grace said, 'Cat's – my sister – is the twenty-seventh. She hates it too. Each year she makes the most incredible *fuss*.' It was a large, round table and June was settled at the place of honor. Simon, sitting next to Grace, ordered his mother a Bloody Mary.

'That's a good idea, honey.'

'They do have good potatoes here.' Adrian scanned the menu. 'I'd almost forgotten. Want some potatoes, June?'

She gave a sour face.

When the waiter came, Adrian ordered for everyone, including a prime rib plus potatoes for June.

'It's not like Gus's, I agree. That's the best place, Grace, in this area. Next time you come, we'll take you there. June loves the scrod.'

'What *is* scrod?' asked Grace. '*Fish?*'

Later, May was mentioned. Grace looked to Simon. 'She must be a recent addition to the McNellises. I've never heard of her.'

'She was married to my younger brother,' said June. 'Babe – the baby in the family. After Caroline. A *second* wife.'

Grace nodded gravely.

'They were married for only two years,' said Adrian.

'Less,' corrected Holly. '*Darlin.*'

'Babe became ill right after they married,' Simon explained. 'And then he died. It's a tragic story, if you think about it.'

Grace asked how he died.

'Don't ask,' barked June. She tapped her cigarette in a small silver ashtray.

Grace's glasses tilted abjectedly to the table. She whispered, 'Oh dear. I've done it again.'

'And ever since then May's been around,' said Marilyn Beth. 'Like a bad smell.'

'At holidays,' said Holly.

'A holiday smell,' said Simon.

'I don't think you're being quite fair.' Adrian was uncomfortable with complaints about his brother's second wife. 'She's a good person and, after all, she's . . . '

'You know what we mean, Adrian.'

'I haven't heard anything unfair,' said June. 'Yet.'

'She doesn't exactly fit, it's true.' Adrian looked about nervously, as if May might rush at the table from any corner. 'You see, Grace, she's very *Southern*.'

'She doesn't sound Southern. She sounds impoverished. Didn't your uncle have insurance?'

'Yup,' said June, tapping her cigarette. 'Lots. And fifty percent of my father's business. May got it all. In cash. She frittered it away. At Odd Lots.'

Grace gaped behind her glasses. 'The discount store?'

'That's a joke,' said Simon. 'She's into shopping. Actually, she bought a small hotel. The money's all gone into that.'

'My father is *spinning*,' said June. 'And Babe in the next plot.'

'She's made mistakes,' said Adrian. 'I'd like to know who *doesn't* make mistakes.'

'With that kind of moolah,' said Marilyn Beth, 'I wouldn't make any mistakes.'

'I saw an interesting article in the *Post*.' Adrian was determined to improve the tone of the conversation. '"All suite" hotels are the rage in New England. I sent it to May. Maybe the trend will go south.'

'Before May's hotel does,' said June.

Waiters descended upon the table. One placed before June a slab of baby-pink beef. She pushed it away.

'How about some deep-fried zucchini, Mom?'

'Honey, I might yip.'

'We should have gone to Gus's.' Adrian was cutting his own prime rib with energy.

'Gus's?' Marilyn Beth's big, fashionable earrings fluttered. 'I hate fish.'

Grace leaned over and patted Marilyn Beth's leather arm. 'I know *exactly* how you feel.'

In the parking lot, as Adrian helped June into the car, the rest of the McNellises watched from a distance.

'I can tell,' said Holly, 'this is her last time out of the house.'

Adrian and June, looking like a married couple, drove slowly away waving. They were followed by Holly and Kevin's Volvo. Simon and Grace offered a birthday drink to Marilyn Beth at Flip's. When they entered, a man at the bar called, 'Yo! Birthday girl!' Marilyn Beth laughed and went to talk to him.

'I have never said "Yo" in my life,' said Simon.

'I was so irritated when I returned from Hong Kong,' said Grace. 'All the stupid talk.'

Marilyn Beth took a chair at their table. 'This place gets all the cokeheads.' She unzipped her leather jacket.

'Cokeheads? At Flip's?' Simon looked around. 'We used to come here in high school.'

The conversation centered around other cancers, as related by the McNellis telephone network. None was relevant. One anecdote offered hope and the next described an extraordinary medical debacle.

'God grant me a car crash,' said Marilyn Beth.

'A *motorcycle* crash,' said Simon.

'Had one already, thanks. God give me insurance next time.'

'You had a motorcycle crash without insurance?' Grace blinked incredulously.

'I had collision. But you can't take collision to the showroom the next day.'

'No, I guess you can't,' said Grace thoughtfully.

'How do you think Mom's taking it, Bethy?'

'Real well.' Marilyn Beth pulled at her thick ponytail. 'She's not depressed or anything. I think she's just waiting to go see Daddy.'

Friends took Marilyn Beth for a birthday night at the bars. Grace remarked, 'She's a sunny soul.'

'Yo!'

'Her last remark astonished me. Is she religious?'

'She's immature, Grace.'

'What does she do again?'

'Mailing lists.'

'Oh.' Grace seemed at a loss for words. Then, unexpectedly, she laughed, showing small teeth. She shook her head. 'I'm sorry. But I have the clearest image of your parents' reunion in heaven. They'd look just like they did in Hong Kong when we'd meet at the Excelsior. Your father would have a big bag slung over his shoulder, wrinkling his jacket.'

'With that little brass bell. He bought it in Japan. You could hear him tinkling for miles.'

'His sports shirt would be buttoned at the top.'

'And Mom would be in slacks and a long shirt . . . '

'With the collar up in the back. And those dangling pearl earrings.'

'Exactly. Imagine heaven looking like the Excelsior lobby. Jammed with Japanese tourists.'

'I used to love seeing them. They were always . . . oh, so much the same.' Grace looked into the distance. She sighed. 'And your mother had the most awful stories about your uncle Adrian's girlfriends. Is that what you call them at that age? Or is it "lady friends?" That sounds dirty.

My mother sends her regards, by the way, and her sympathies. Not sympathies. That's premature I guess.' Grace's brow wrinkled. She tilted her head and looked at Simon. 'Her *prayers?*'

They talked about the McNellis attitude toward the illness. No medical details were spared June; no surreptitious conversations were held behind doors. When the children related information on the telephone, they raised their voices to emphasize that June was still around, still a participant no matter how removed. They rejected the condescension shown to ill people, although they had little choice: condescension toward June McNellis, even a diminished version, was unimaginable.

'Indeed,' said Grace. 'She always was a bit strong. The whole McNellis family.'

'Not strong,' said Simon. 'Perfect. That's what the town always said. That's what we believed. Mom fed it to us.'

Grace looked down at her Tab.

'What's the matter?'

Grace sighed. 'Well, you know how I feel about you and your family.'

Silence descended.

'That year in Hong Kong . . . '

'I know,' said Simon. 'You always thought the McNellises were too important to me.'

The bar had filled up. Marilyn Beth's characterization had been correct. The waiters were the yuppies. The customers were unshaven, beer-bellied louts.

'Marilyn Beth is amazing.' Grace used a revived tone. 'She acts no differently. Holly is changed, I think. More busy and less . . . subdued.'

'Mother hen.'

'Yes. That's it.'

'This is a big event for Holly,' Simon said. 'She'll turn into the new June McNellis.'

45

Grace paused. 'I can't tell about you, Simon. How are you holding up?'

To Simon the question summoned a single image: his mother lying in bed, radio blasting, gazing up with an odd, alert look. Simon had found an unchanged mother on his return home: unchanged at the dining-room table, in family conversations, when she engaged in the traditional repartee. But the mother in the bedroom was different. Partly it was the pity she showed for Simon and his sisters – a pity that none had thought decent to accept. But Simon discerned something more: an urgency, a searching look, a plaintive tone. But what about? When he left the sickroom, he often went into the bathroom to look at himself in the mirror and think: What?

'I'll buy some cigarettes.'

'Oh, Simon.'

'Only when I'm drunk.' He returned and lit up. 'You've heard so much about my perfect family over the years. I wanted you to know something more. I haven't told anyone else. Not Holly, not anyone. Mom and I had a knock-down drag-out fight two years ago. When she came to India.'

'I thought that trip went perfectly.'

'Almost.'

From Simon's verandah, three floors up, one could view strollers at almost all hours. Guards in turbans, skinny houseboys darting from house to house in white, stained trousers. One shouted. Three laughed. Sunset was expiring and on the lot next door – a house going up, a brick silhouette over fading royal blue – an off-duty worker played a languorous bamboo flute. They sat beneath tall potted trees, which shook and then stilled as the evening breeze turned to the still night of north India. The stars overhead were bright. On the table between them, on its glass top, were ridiculously tall bottles of beer. June announced her plan to sell the house to his sister. More room was needed, as everyone knew; Jeremy's school, and Paul's before you knew it. She would move to a condominium or reside upstairs in a bedroom converted at her expense. Holly would need an early inheritance. And even then, she would have money problems. An arrangement was necessary with Simon and Marilyn: a long-term loan, a commitment, some use of their shares of June's estate. Simon called it unfair. June, who rejected partiality and unfairness, spoke unyieldingly. The night raged on, the bottles multiplied, the street actually emptied. The guards snored in their chairs. The flute stopped abruptly. Simon never recalled going to sleep. But he remembered his mother tearless and firm. The next morning, there were averted glances. She left for Hong Kong the following day. 'You're just being greedy,' she had said, standing. 'Your own interests – that's all you're thinking of. You of all of us, Simon.'

'I do remember that. "You of all of us." ' He lit another cigarette. 'Us McNellises. That's what she meant.'

'All over the house? Over money?'

'To her it was about the house. But not money. She became obsessed with the idea of the house going to Holly. It was right after Daddy died . . . '

'Yes.'

' . . . and Mom had changed. I wondered if the girls saw it. Her whole solar system, for the first time, was wobbling. And this was her way of stabilizing it. I had the unpleasant task of scotching the plan.'

'Was it really so bitter?'

'Unbelievable.'

'I just can't imagine your mother fighting. That didn't seem her way. With one of you. With *you*.'

'She had to convince me. Then everyone else would have fallen in line. I forced her into a corner when I said it was unfair: June McNellis, the paragon of fairness. So she tried to bully me. I understood it all the next day. The two of us are so much alike, as everyone says.'

A scuffle arose at the bar. A bare-chested man was pushed onto the floor. A girl with wild hair threw her hand in the air and yelled an obscenity. A fresh-faced waiter rushed over.

'Last year on home leave, Holly and Kevin's plans had changed. They decided to re-do the attic in their own house. Mom mentioned, in passing, that if they ever did take the house it would have to be fair to me and Marilyn Beth. I took that as an apology.'

'You were wise.' Grace jiggled the ice and stared into her Tab. 'Were you jealous? That Holly was getting the house? And your mother?'

'Not jealous,' said Simon. 'That wasn't the point, Grace.'

'Had you and your mother ever fought before?'

'Once.'

'So bitterly?'

Simon nodded.

'*Really?*'

Simon lit another cigarette. 'More so.'

Grace had an amazed look. 'You've never told me.'

Simon shook his head. '*That* was long, long ago. And far, far away.'

At the station, Simon pulled into a parking space beneath the platform. Grace sighed and leaned over to give a slow, weak hug.

'I'd like to come into the city one night next week.'

'Of course,' said Grace. She stared through the windshield and exhaled. 'Oh well,' she said. She gathered her things and walked slowly up the ramp, scolding her black umbrella. The train pulled away with gaudy brilliance in the drizzly night.

At home, Adrian was watching the news in the greenhouse. Simon reminded him they had to buy a Christmas tree. And of May's arrival on Monday.

'Next time I vote for Gus's,' Adrian said. 'June loves the – wait! Here's something from the Middle East.'

Simon closed down the house. He walked to his mother's room and found the lights on. She shifted and smiled at him.

'Hi.'

'Hi.' With an effort, June leaned and turned down the radio. 'Was Adrian upset? That I couldn't eat?'

'He's sure you could have eaten scrod.'

June chuckled. 'He's wrong.'

'I feel sorry for him. First Babe, then Daddy and Grandpa. Now you.'

'He never thought he'd get old. Or we'd get old.'

Simon stood by the white wicker dresser. He motioned to the picture of his father in the water. 'Is this the Delaware?' He picked up a silver scalloped dish. A florid 'M' was inscribed in the center.

'It's sterling. It was your grandmother McNellis's.'

'I've never noticed it before.'

'Take it.' June stared at Simon. 'Put it in your bag and take it back to India. It'll look good with your things.'

'No, Mom. That's unnecessary. It's not the time.'

'The girls have gotten other things. In drips and drabs.'

'No Mom. Later.'

Simon leaned against the door. 'Are you afraid Mom? Of dying?'

'No, honey. I'm not. It sounds strange but it's true. I am afraid of suffering. And of hospitals. And about you all.'

'We know that.'

'Did you discuss the living will with Holly?' June shifted and grimaced. 'Maybe I ought to have another pill, honey. The painkiller.'

When he returned with the pill, June again turned down the radio.

'Holly and Kevin haven't decided about the house, I gather.'

'No.' She sighed. 'Those two. But it has to be fair to you and Marilyn Beth. You know that, don't you?'

'I know Mom.'

'I don't know if they can afford it. And I don't care anymore. Maybe they should find another house. This isn't the only house in the world.' June leaned over and turned up the radio. A black voice complained about racism.

No light showed under the door of the girls' room, where Adrian slept. Simon plucked lotion from his toiletry kit and began his nightly masturbation. In the darkness of the room the windows glowed. Car lights illuminated the tops of the wet trees. He arranged his briefs just below the scrotum and concentrated on scenes from his erotic past. He closed his eyes, summoning far-flung places and half-remembered women. But Simon's effort failed. His eyes remained open, staring at the trees that were more familiar to him than any others. Finally, he surrendered to a woman with black hair falling on disheveled bedding. With the treetops, he saw *tatami* mats, a light dangling from a low ceiling, a distinct curve of skin and back. From the past, he heard a special moan. He tried to join it. He labored to keep the bed from rattling. It was the same whenever Simon was in his mother's house: as if the house stocked for him one memory only and wouldn't let him free.

They had waited too long to buy a tree. Adrian paced the local nursery, clapping gloves and emitting steamy disparagements. He lifted the branch of a poor specimen and, meaningfully, let it flop. A tree was finally selected and, with manly curses, installed in the usual corner of June's living-room. But no one was around to help festoon it. Simon searched the frigid upstairs closet for lights and bulbs. The closet served as the McNellis attic; it ran along the back of the house, behind the two upstairs bedrooms and their bathrooms, accessible from each through small louvered doors. Simon hadn't penetrated it deeply since childhood: its tall cardboard boxes filled with stained bedspreads; his grandfather's stately cologne bottle, showing an inch of ancient yellow liquid; lonely battalions of old clothes. By mid-afternoon, the tree was finished. Simon retrieved the cassette player from his father's den and, after another chilly search, found the Christmas tapes.

Andy Williams was smile-singing when Holly pushed through the front door at dusk. 'This is wonderful! Oh, Simon: it's the best thing to happen to the house in weeks!'

'What did you expect?'

'I dreaded this!' The two boys pushed past her to the greenhouse television. 'That's why I didn't come over. I thought it would be *such* a downer.'

'I tried calling you. And Marilyn Beth.'

'I'm sure she's deeply hungover.'

June was also cheered by the tree. She gazed at it from the wheelchair and pointed out the visible wires. It was one of her good nights. She had two Bloody Marys and nibbled at the scrod Adrian brought in from Gus's. The two of them talked about childhood friends. One had sent a moving letter.

On Sunday, Simon found a casserole on the front stoop with a card from the young couple next to Vera Sherman's. Later that evening there was a bottle of champagne from Judge Houlihan, one of the local democrats. It was tied with a gay red ribbon.

'I can't believe this food thing,' Simon said. 'It's as if we lived on the prairie.'

'The Smythes left the most awful pasta,' said June. 'Holly said there was tuna in it.'

'They must have to sneak up the hill.' Simon peered out the front window. 'They don't think of ringing the bell?'

'Thank God for that,' said June.

'Somehow champagne seems *in*appropriate,' commented Adrian. 'They must think you're swinging from the chandeliers, June.'

She laughed.

'Some people just can't take the *hard* truths,' Adrian said. 'They must look on the *bright* side. Whoopee! Cancer!'

Simon opened the champagne.

'Ain't we got fun?' exulted Adrian. 'Yeah! More anti-nausea pills!'

But June couldn't take the carbonation. Simon chucked the casserole after bringing it to the table for June to inspect. 'It has tuna too.' She probed with a butter knife. 'Never understood that.'

The weatherman had a prediction, finally. June wanted

the sound turned up. He announced a chance of snow at Christmas.

'Oh wouldn't that be perfect.' June stared to the back window and the yard beyond, which was yellowed and bare.

Simon looked across the table at Holly. Her wide eyes were filled with tears.

'Okay, Mom.' He rose from the table. 'What can I tempt you with? Some Clamato and a pancake? Bacon?'

June stared through the window, as if waiting for the snow to begin. 'Yes honey. A pancake sounds good.'

Christmas shopping for June was a dilemma. Simon, Holly, Marilyn Beth and Adrian went to the mall.

'I didn't want to bring something beautiful from India,' Simon said. 'I'd just inherit it in a few months.' Marilyn Beth, half-joking, said that was her idea of the perfect gift. Holly scolded her for sounding greedy. In the same way, expensive presents for June were inappropriate, permanent things, clothes, jewelry and jokes. No present could require an alteration in the house, as a painting would, or furniture. Even books were out: June's reading habit had drained away.

'I thought Dad was hard to buy for at a hundred and two,' said Adrian. 'Maybe we should take inspiration from Judge Houlihan. Do they sell streamers here? Noise-makers?'

Holly already had her present: a video containing all the McNellis home movies. Marilyn Beth emerged from a store with an enormous piece of blue foam with seismic bumps. 'We can cut this up. You know the trouble she has getting comfortable in that chair? And it'll look big under the tree.'

Simon bought June's favorite candy. 'I have something back at the house,' he said. 'Something small.' Adrian was the last to choose and the most satisfied on the way home.

Everyone praised his ingenuity. He bought a cordless tele-phone. 'June can take all her calls now, right at the dining-room table.'

'I wouldn't bet on that,' said Holly.

When they pushed through the red door, Marilyn Beth shouted 'Don't look!' and hustled the foam mattress into the den. The others swung their shopping bags through the living-room. June was at the dining-room table but she wasn't alone. To her left, in Marilyn Beth's place, was a small woman with flapper-style hair, jet black, the ends twisted up before her ears. Her hands, tiny and white, danced excitedly on the table. They darted back and forth between herself and the sick woman.

'*Hello* darlins!' The woman, remaining seated, swiveled to the newcomers with eager eyes thick with makeup. 'You've been *shoppin*!' She clasped her hands to her bony chest.

From the rear Simon could perceive June's sag. 'Hello May,' he said. 'When did you get in?'

'Why, thirty minutes ago darlin. I took a taxi.'

'Hello May,' said Adrian. Kisses were exchanged. 'How was the trip? I hope Kevin wasn't supposed to pick you up.'

'I took a taxi, darlin. When I got off the train and looked all around and saw absolutely no one I knew, I just flagged one of these station wagon thingies.'

In the kitchen, Holly whispered to Simon, 'Kevin would be so mad!'

'We've been havin the most *wonderful* talk,' said May. 'Mum and me. I'm tellin her about the fascinatin people I met on the train. I was just gettin out their business cards. One of them thought he knew you Adrian.'

'Really?' Adrian looked puzzled. 'Don't look, June.'

'I won't.'

'I'm starved,' Simon called. 'Mom? What'll you have?'

'I don't know, honey.'

54

'I'll make another pancake.'

'I saved some clippings for you, May, upstairs.' Adrian closed the top of his shopping bag, folding it several times. 'We had great success at the mall, June. And I don't mind telling you that even Dad was easier to buy for.'

'Doc *loved* the rocker Babe and I bought him,' said May. 'That was the year before Babe died. It was a JFK rocker.'

'It's been molding in the shed since the day it arrived.' June made a heavy motion toward the back window.

May's eyes wrinkled with black sadness. 'Why's that, darlin?'

June shrugged. 'Take it if you want. Ship it. Better arrange it this trip.'

'Simon wanted to buy a case of champagne,' Adrian said. 'And some hula hoops. Judge Houlihan recommended them.' This led to a reprise of the champagne story. Marilyn Beth said she went to school with Judge Houlihan's son, whom she called 'Studman of the tenth grade.' The repartee continued from kitchen to dining-room until the whole family was seated with a lunch before them. Or the whole family minus one. May darted in from the greenhouse carrying an armload of laundry.

'May?' asked Simon. 'What are you doing?'

'What do you mean, darlin?'

'Those are my clothes.'

'Oh, I'm just extendin a helpin hand.' May dumped the wrinkled clothes on the round table. She plucked out a heelless blue sock. 'I always help Mum like this. Something to keep my hands busy.'

Simon removed his laundry from the dining-room.

'Simon's taken over,' said June.

'And he can be quite the martinet,' said Adrian. 'Especially on the subject of dirty pans.'

'You should see his dinners.' June fumbled for a cigarette.

May's eyes, inquisitive and innocent, followed Simon. When he returned to his place at the table she said, 'Why, sure darlin. I'll find somethin else to keep my hands occupied. I'm sure there are *millions* of things that need doin. That's always the case when somebody gets, you know.'

'Cancer,' said June.

From the greenhouse, a small boy's voice called, 'What's for lunch, Mom? I'm hungry, Mom.'

'You can come to my house, May,' said Marilyn Beth. 'God did I feel thirty yesterday!'

'Miss First Nighter,' said Holly.

'What was Daddy's awful sneer when Bethy threw up in the Vega?'

June coughed, her hand in the air.

'*Don't*,' pleaded Marilyn Beth. 'Daddy was bad enough. I had the runs *and* the most incredible headache.'

June finished coughing and pushed aside her plate, containing an uneaten pancake. 'Mary-Loads-Of-Fun,' she said. 'That's what Don called her.'

'For my whole goddamned senior year!'

In the afternoon, Simon pulled pork chops from the freezer. They were rock-hard. He looked accusingly at the clock, poked the meat and cursed. Turning, he found Vera Sherman grinning in the kitchen doorway. 'Mrs Sherman!' As always, she stood stock still, her calm, white sneakers neatly together. She looked neither young nor old and Simon couldn't recall her ever looking otherwise. The cropped ginger hair, the peach lipstick, the pursed, wry smile beneath it.

She handed him a cake. 'I saw May arrive this morning. I just stopped her at the bottom of the driveway. We had a chat. I was shivering. But I enjoyed every minute.'

'She went shopping. We hope we won't see her until the stores close.'

'Pathmark is open twenty-four hours.' Vera giggled guiltily.

June's thump sounded and Simon excused himself. When he returned, Vera was at the table with a glass of iced tea. 'The fairies are back?'

'I'm making it now. Every morning. It goes bad within a day or two.'

'It gets those awful stringy things.'

'Mom can't drink anything else. Except some Clamato. Here she is.'

June walked laboriousiy through the living-room, grimacing every few steps. She settled gingerly in her chair. Simon circled the living-room turning on lights.

'Hello Vera.' June panted. The buttons on her shirt were askew. Skin flaked around her mouth. She tried unsuccessfully to smooth her creased white hair.

'How are you June?'

'Not so good. These pills are making it *worse*. I often wish Ross was around, Vera, to give advice at least.'

'He was always so critical of the medication for cancer patients. He said none of the other doctors cared. For, you know . . . '

'Terminals. He was right. Don't forget the back drapes, honey.'

Adrian was napping so May could be discussed.

'She said a strange thing to me,' Vera related. 'I *had* to ask about Ruthie. And May took the car out of gear and even turned off the ignition. She told me she was worried about Ruthie's finances. Her eyes got very wide: you know how they do?'

Simon imitated her expression.

'She said Ruthie's money might be running out.'

'It is.' June lit a cigarette. 'But it's nothing to do with May.'

'I knew *that*.'

'She's after Ruthie's money. I thought so.'

'How?' Simon's tone was shocked.

'The will would have to be changed,' June said. 'Adrian's the trustee.'

'How much is there?'

'Nothing.'

'So what's the . . . ?'

'To May every penny counts. And she doesn't know nothing's left.'

'Has May gone through all that money?' Vera asked. 'From your father?'

'Yup.' June grimaced again. 'Honey, could you get me my pill? There's a new prescription in the bathroom.'

Simon returned with a furious expression. 'Have you seen the medicine closet? It's been wiped out!'

'It's May,' June sighed. 'She was in there while you were napping. She said she cleaned out the towels and sheets too.'

'What's she doing going through our closets? Daddy's shaving stuff is gone.'

June shrugged.

'Is she staying in the den again?' asked Vera. 'I noticed the lights.'

June explained that May liked the downstairs den because it gave her control over the entire house. To claim the room as her own, she left clothes in its closet.

'May's clothes are in the attic closet,' said Simon.

'She leaves something in every closet and drawer. Like a dog marking out its territory.'

Vera giggled girlishly.

'Her territory?' Simon asked. 'What territory?'

June indicated the entire house.

'Ross's mother used to do that too,' said Vera. 'I'd find her in my basement. She was crazy for our bank statements. And jewelry. I never recovered that bracelet. Remember that bracelet, June? With the coins?'

'Thank the Lord she didn't have taste.'

Vera laughed. 'I could have lost everything if you think of it!'

May was still out when Dr Coughlin visited. He examined June in her bedroom. When he returned he was shaking his head. 'This is not a good situation,' he said.

Holly asked some questions about the medication. Adrian added his comments. Simon, after some hemming and hawing, asked how long his mother had. Coughlin said anywhere from six to ten weeks. His voice dropped to a whisper: 'There's definite liver involvement. *Definite*.'

When he was gone, Simon said: 'Do you think he told Mom about the liver?'

'It didn't sound like it,' said Holly.

Adrian paced from kitchen to dining-room, shaking his head and pursing his lips.

'I don't know if we should tell her,' said Holly. 'Not after Daddy. She'll start worrying about her bilirubin and all that.'

Simon and Adrian agreed, although the decision made all three nervous. They hadn't held anything back from June before.

Simon went for Christmas Eve drinks with friends. On his return, he passed Vera Sherman's darkened house. The McNellis ground floor looked equally shut down, including the darkened windows of the den, where May was staying. But when he stepped in the door, Simon heard the eternal voices of the call-in radio shows. June's bedroom lights blazed. She turned down the radio and squinted at the blue digits on the clock.

'You're early.'

'They have to wake up tomorrow. We put together an incredibly complicated dinosaur. You want fresh water?' He fetched it. 'It's snowing Mom. It looks like you got your wish.'

59

'That's wonderful. It's going to be a fine Christmas.'
June got an ashamed look on her face. 'I had to be wheeled
into my room tonight. I asked Adrian. I just couldn't make
it.'

'Coughlin was really vague about this medication.'
Simon heard a sound outside the room. He stepped into
the hall to find May descending the stairs quickly and
softly.

'Why hello darlin.' She gave her bright look: the charming Southern belle, arm on the banister, youth buried
beneath decades of mascara. 'I was havin the most *wonderful* time looking through the picture box. There are
some precious photos which I've never *seen*.' Her petite
hands, clumsy and white from the cold air of the attic,
held a jumble of color photos. 'See, here's Babe on the
beach. It must be the Hamptons. We ought to all go
through them one of these nights. Maybe tomorrow? A
Christmas treat?'

'The picture box is in the very back of the attic.'

'I knew you wouldn't mind. Adrian's snorin away. I
was listenin for you and I put everything back just where
it was. These are duplicates, darlin, someone had *lots* of
copies made. You don't mind if I take these, Simon darlin?
You want to see the others?'

Simon climbed the stairs to his room and stooped
through the small, louvered attic door. Everything was as
he had seen it the previous day except for the picture box.
It sat in the middle of the closet with torn orange envelopes, plastic bags, snapshots and negatives protruding
violently from the top. He pushed the pictures back and
placed the box behind a rack of stiff summer dresses. The
closet was so cold he could see his breath. When he started
his nightly masturbation, a stray thought stalled him. He
walked across the room, cock bobbing heavily, and locked
the bedroom door.

Again, he was transported to that particular Japanese

room. To bring himself back, he summoned his adolescence and his premier self-stimulations. He could recall only one of the mental objects: a girl who had been forced to leave town when her mother died. The sight of the bathroom provided another memory: of the nights he'd try on condoms for stimulation, only to rip them off, thick and musty, to achieve climax. He had stashed a collection of condoms in the wall behind the built-in dresser, along with pornography, alcohol, marijuana pipes. Some secret artifacts were still there. In memory, Simon could see the white paper bag from the pharmacy, heavy with condoms, slumped on the bathroom sink in the yellowed light of the old bathroom. But everything was changed now: June had renovated. He also recalled masturbating with his legs propped up against the wall. That too was in the past: the bed had been shifted to a different position.

Simon didn't want his mother alone at the dining-room table on Christmas morning. But when he descended, she was still in bed. Her bedroom lights gave off a tired, yellow blaze. The radio bellowed.

In the kitchen, infused with bluish light from the greenhouse, Simon found May spreading jam on a crumbly muffin. She wore a flannel nightgown with a tear in the collar. Her evening makeup had melted, causing earthquake destruction on her aged-doll face.

'Merry Christmas darlin! Doesn't the tree look just *wonderful* with all those, oh, I'd say *three million* presents?' Adrian ambled in behind Simon. 'What time does the gang arrive? Do I have time for a jog?'

'No jogging this morning,' said Simon. 'Look!'

It had snowed overnight. Through the greenhouse, it obscured the trees, the garden, even the back fence. The world outside was reduced to white humps under a sparkling dry blanket.

Simon woke June. 'They'll be here in a half hour. How do you feel?'

She blinked up from the pillow. 'Pretty good, honey, I think.'

'Three inches,' Simon said, 'and still snowing. Merry Christmas, Mom.'

June dressed with special care. She wore her father's navy-blue cardigan with the leather buttons. At the table, she asked for a pancake.

'You make the best pancakes, honey. Compared to the girls.'

'Mom, you taught us all.'

'Well, something happened. Holly's are too . . . crispy. And Marilyn Beth's are too thick. She's too lazy to get the consistency right.'

Simon looked down at the frying circle of batter. He prodded it. 'You've psyched me out, Mom. This one's going to be crispy or thick.'

May returned, hair damp and freshly made up. She wore a black skirt and matching jacket. 'Good mornin June darlin merry, *merry* Christmas.' She pecked at the top of June's head and straightened quickly. Her small white hands flew to her ears, pinching in place the loops of shiny, black hair. 'June darlin, don't you want one of these *wonderful* oat-bran muffins I bought for you at the Food Emporium?'

'I've never eaten an oat-bran muffin in my life.'

'Oat-bran,' said Adrian. 'Good for your health, June. Your cholesterol.'

'My *cholesterol*?'

'Darlin they are *real good*. And I don't know what to do with this last one. How about you Adrian?'

'I might have some of this bacon.' He smiled his charming smile. 'Even cholesterol takes a holiday.'

'Simon darlin?'

Simon declined. He delivered June's pancake. 'Thank you honey. It looks perfect.'

'In that case,' said May, 'I might as well! After all, if cholesterol's takin a holiday!' She gave a false girlish giggle. The door pushed open and the boys rushed into the house. Jeremy showed June his Batman watch. Paul said, 'I'm hungry, Mom. What's for breakfast, Mom?' He looked around, mouth open, and ran back to the front door. He called into the falling snow. 'Mom? What's for *breakfast*?'

Holly and Kevin came in, wiping shoes. Kevin grumbled: 'Five-thirty!' The children were allowed to search for their presents under the tree. Adrian collected orders for Bloody Marys. June told Simon to telephone Marilyn Beth but the door opened and Marilyn Beth buffaloed into the living-room, pale and puffy-eyed. Her long, thick hair was pulled into a sloppy ponytail.

'I think I see another Bloody Mary customer,' said Adrian.

'Shooters at the Mug. Then the Five Points. Merry Christmas Mom.' Marilyn Beth kissed June on the lips as she had since childhood. 'I'm *sure* your tolerance decreases with age.' She ripped off her leather jacket.

'Your father's didn't,' said June. 'Not for alcohol or sex.'

'Why that's *interestin* darlin,' said May. 'Now, Don *was* the manly type . . . '

'I don't want to hear it,' said Marilyn Beth. But May continued. 'Poor Babe, you know, after he got sick the first time . . . '

Adrian quashed May's monologue with Bloody Mary deliveries. May refused a drink and disappeared suddenly through the living-room.

'Thank you Adrian,' said June. 'Marilyn, you know what I would consider the *best* Christmas present?'

'What Mom?'

'If you got that hair cut.'

Everyone at the table groaned. 'It's Christmas,' complained Holly.

'A mother's last wish.'

'Actually, I'm ready to do it,' said Marilyn Beth. 'And not to satisfy you, Mom, if you must know. I have the place. I think I know the style.'

'I'm so sick of seeing that hair dripping down. You could be *so* pretty. No permanent, I hope.'

'Just on top.'

'Oh God,' groaned June. 'The rat's nest.'

'I get permanents, Mom.' Holly tousled her blonde curls.

'You're different.'

May reappeared, small arms filled with tissue-wrapped presents. 'I *like* Marilyn's hair. I think it's *wonderful*! I wish *I* had hair like hers.'

'It's a pain to wash,' Marilyn Beth muttered. 'Where are my presents? On this side?'

The distribution of presents began. Holly read the tags and Simon delivered them. A small pile rose in front of June, who sat smoking and watching the rest of the family. Marilyn Beth ripped open her gifts and shouted excited thanks.

'May?' Simon handed her a package.

'Why thank you darlin.'

'Sime,' called Adrian. 'I've been meaning to read this! It got great reviews.'

Everyone gathered around and June opened her presents. First came the cordless telephone, which Adrian immediately began assembling. Then Marilyn Beth's mattress, which burst from its wrapping paper. May's present was a book called *Decorating Rich*.

'I just want to sit with Mum for a long time and flip along lookin at all these *wonderful* houses.' Her quick hands manipulated the pages. 'Look at this one darlin. Cowboy style!'

The three children exchanged glances. Adrian saw them and, in a guilty tone, made loud comments about intricate modern telephones.

'This one is from Simon,' June announced. She tore through the wrapping. Underneath was a framed, embroidered piece of cloth.

'Read it, Simon,' called Adrian.

'It's Indian. From the Vedas.' Simon cleared his throat:

That eyelike sun, may we be seeing it for a hundred autumns,
May we live a hundred autumns,
May we delight and rejoice for a hundred autumns,
May we be in our places for a hundred autumns,
May we be hearing and speaking for a hundred autumns,
May we be unvanquished for a hundred autumns.
May we be able to see this sun for a long time.

'I wasn't sure it was right,' he said.

'It would have been perfect for Doc,' said Adrian. 'We could have changed a hundred to a hundred and two.'

'May,' said Holly. 'You're in every line.'

'This embroidery would look gorgeous on a shirt.' Marilyn Beth tilted the frame to catch the light from the back window.

'It's beautiful, honey,' said June. 'We've gotten such beautiful things from your part of the world. If only Don could have seen India.'

'He would have loved it darlin,' said May. 'Babe always wanted to go to India. But then he got sick . . . '

June's final present was a small rectangular box: Holly's videotape. There were immediate calls to watch it. June was moved into Don's recliner in the greenhouse. The tape was a swift succession of super-eight films, sprocket holes visible between reels, which bounced chronologically between decades. 'The numb nuts got them mixed up,' Kevin cried. 'I marked them clearly!' But the randomness added to the video. Marilyn Beth was a teen, then a white-haired toddler. June's salt-and-pepper hair kept shifting shades, the style changeless. Simon's pimples loomed at ten times the normal size. Each member of the family alternated between flushed embarrassment and noisy delight. The greenhouse rang with protests in all voices.

'Who's that?' asked Jeremy.

'It's your Mommy,' said Simon.

Paul stared with open mouth.

The younger June was there, of course, holding hands outside church with tiny children and lying on chaise-longues at poolsides, mouthing silent imprecations. The children wore school uniforms, bathing suits, communion outfits of white and graduation robes of crimson or black. They fell slowly into snowdrifts. They shooed the camera away with smiles gone gray with braces. Marilyn was consistently pudgy. Simon was manic with feminine gestures. Holly was forever glued to the backgrounds. The films from the famed summer in the Dominican Republic were the most acclaimed and the most beautiful. Their colors had remained fast while the others had washed out.

'Daddy was *handsome*,' said Marilyn Beth. 'Not fat at all.'

'Look at this one, June,' said Adrian. 'You lost all that weight that summer.' The beautiful woman on the screen waved; her hair was still dark.

'God you were skinny, Mom,' said Marilyn Beth.

'It didn't last,' said June.

'Why look,' cried May. 'There's my Babe. With a beard! I didn't know he visited you in the Dominican Republic.'

'With Caroline,' said June. As if on cue, a dark-haired woman in a rich swimsuit laughed a silent, horsy laugh.

'There's Peter darlin,' exclaimed May. 'With a fish!'

66

The next scene showed a swimming-pool surrounded by undulating banana trees. A fat man did a half-gainer from a diving-board.

'Who the hell is that?' laughed Adrian. 'Why, it's *Orson Welles*. Were you a friend of Orson's, June? I preferred Rita myself.'

'It's Charlie Mozena. He worked with Don in Santo Domingo. Remember Charlie, Holly? Simon? Marilyn was too young.'

Even Adrian was disconcerted when he swam, lithe and handsome, across a glary lake. Meeting him at the shore was a petite woman with slanted eyes. 'I remember *her*,' said Holly. 'And her little dog.' Adrian stammered an update. She lived in Washington; a child was at Stanford.

June's reaction to the films was hard to gauge. She made the usual remarks through breaths of cigarette smoke. But Simon perceived something hidden in her tone. He wondered if the videotape had been a good idea.

It ended abruptly. 'I didn't know Daddy was such a hunk,' said Marilyn Beth. 'What happened?' May touched a tissue to the corners of her black eyes. 'It's so wonderful to see my Babe walkin around and bein, oh, *healthy*!' She snorted suddenly. 'Caroline laughs *too* much. Even Babe said so.'

June retired to her room. The house settled into the usual Christmas-day lethargy. Adrian went jogging. Holly prepared lunch for the boys. Simon fiddled with a labyrinth. 'I had the same thing when I was a kid,' he said. 'But it was wood, not plastic. And it didn't have batteries.'

'I like batteries,' said Jeremy. 'Let me.'

'Let *me*,' said Paul.

Kevin agreed to drop May at the train station. She was spending a few days in the city with Peter, the only child of Babe and Caroline. Holly labored over Christmas dinner. The menu was only slightly changed from previous years. 'Nobody likes creamed onions, anyway,' she said.

Simon slowly ironed the cloth for the round table. He found a stain; Holly said a dish would cover it.

'Is that how Mom would have handled this?'

'Yes, Simon. That stain is fifteen years old.' Next to the table was June's pile of presents. Holly picked up *Decorating Rich*. 'Look at this.'

'Let's throw that fucking book away,' said Simon.

'It's shampoo time,' Holly said. 'Maybe I can get Mom into something special.'

Marilyn Beth arrived and Adrian started pouring drinks. June made her entrance through the living-room wearing a familiar shirtwaist dress in blue shot silk. It was the first dress she had worn in weeks.

'I feel pretty proud of myself,' she said. 'I feel pretty good.'

The cordless telephone warbled. It was Barbara. Holly mentioned steroids and held the phone away from her. Barbara's laugh rasped through the air. Marilyn Beth made pretend she was grabbing the phone and said, in an imitation of May, ' "I'll get it *darlin*." I can't stand the way she dominates the goddamned telephone.'

'Hey, wait a minute,' said Adrian. 'I don't like these bad vibes towards May and I think we ought to cut it out. She is, after all, family. And that counts. I mean none of us are perfect.'

'Okay, uncle,' said Marilyn Beth. Simon and Holly nodded contritely.

'I don't know,' June announced from the wheelchair. 'I'm sick to death of this bran muffin crap and I wish she'd go home. She's not really family, Adrian, she was married to Babe for barely two years. And he was sick. In the *head*.'

'June, that's not true!'

She flexed her chin to the ceiling. 'Believe what you want. But that's how I feel. And it's my house, my family and *my* last Christmas. She doesn't belong here no matter what you say. It was a mistake. Furthermore – no, never mind. Honey, get me a refill, will you?'

Simon had rented a video to distract the boys during their early dinner. It was *Bye Bye Birdie*. One by one the McNellis children were lured to the greenhouse by the familiar songs. Adrian joined them and commented appreciatively on Ann-Margret. When Conrad Birdie arrived at the town square holding his guitar like a machine gun, Holly instructed the boys: 'Watch the girls, Jeremy. They're going to faint.'

Marilyn Beth sat on the arm of the recliner. Simon stood with a beer in his hand. Holly knelt with the children on the floor. All three started swaying to the song. Simon bellowed: 'You . . . gotta be . . . sincere!'

'It's much funnier than I remember,' said Holly. 'What happened to our record?'

'I lent it to Joanne,' replied Marilyn Beth. 'She never returned it.'

The beat picked up. Conrad Birdie stepped off the central fountain and a ring of women fainted. Marilyn Beth yelled: 'There goes the mayor's wife!'

'What's fainting, Mom?' asked Paul.

At the dining-room table, June McNellis pushed away her wine glass. She labored to her feet and grasped her cane. She walked to the dining-room doorway and stood at the topmost step, looking down into the darkened greenhouse. The deep blue snow was visible through the invisible panes.

We know what June McNellis saw physically: six faces trained in one direction, catching the liquid light of video. We know what she concentrated on: three of those faces, an adult update of those black-and-white photo groupings that had ceased when her children discovered pimples and self-consciousness. But what June McNellis really saw we'll never know precisely.

'Here Mom. Take the recliner.'

'No, don't move. I'm enjoying you from here.' The lights backed June, infusing her soft, clean hair with a white shine. Her face was a shadow.

What was the effect of the old film echoing its noises down corridors that had heard them many, many times, many years before? What came back in echo, registering on the faces of the McNellis children? Did June McNellis find mere nostalgia in the darkened, converted greenhouse? Sibling togetherness? Or was she taken by a double image: the McNellis children grown large, handsome and complete, with faces cleansed of time's blemishes – its tics, its affectations, the muddy bootprints of the harsh outside world? Did June see her offspring as she had so often dreamt them: physically fulfilled but in all other ways arrested? Was this every mother's unspoken dream: children who grow but don't change? Who roam but never actually stray? Simon twitched his hips, adolescently thin in blue jeans. Marilyn Beth facetiously swung her thick ponytail. Holly, with Paul on her lap, sang in a soft choir-girl's voice.

The song ended. A bell rang in the kitchen. Holly jumped up and Simon said, 'I'll help.' Marilyn Beth said, 'Mom, come sit.'

'No honey, I enjoyed watching that one song.' She moved back to her place at the table, head down, expression unseen. When the movie lost its grip, Marilyn Beth and Adrian returned to the dining-room. June said, 'The first thing I want tossed is your father's damn recliner.'

The dinner went well, although June sagged midway. Simon said, 'There's a spot on this tablecloth.' June said, 'I know, honey.' Adrian asked several times about the creamed onions, which were his Christmas favorite.

'I bumped into Judge Houlihan at the video store,' said Simon.

Adrian looked up eagerly. 'The champagne king? The cancer *bon vivant?*'

'He asked after you, Mom. He shook his head and thrust out his lip. Like this.' Simon imitated. 'He said Marjorie wanted to pay you a visit.'

'I'll be in bed,' said June.

'She has some balloons,' said Adrian. 'Castanets.' He made a Bronx cheer. 'Party records.'

'But then he said she couldn't come over because she's sick too. I figured you forgot to tell me. I said I was sorry and asked if it was serious.'

'It is,' said Adrian. 'They've gone through four crates of champagne already.'

'The carbonation nearly made me yip.' June lit a cigarette.

'He looked pretty grim,' Simon continued. 'And said, "She has a cold." '

'Jesus Christ.' June exhaled blue smoke.

'A cold?' said Holly.

'People are such asses,' said June.

'But when she recovers, apparently, her first stop is right here, Mom.'

'Now, June,' said Adrian, 'if Judge Houlihan was kind enough to send French champagne over here, Mrs Houlihan obviously deserves something for her cold. I think she rates a can of Schlitz.'

Adrian wouldn't let it go and for the rest of the night told Judge Houlihan jokes. 'This man,' he said, 'shouldn't be a *judge.* I'm writing the board. He should be director of the hospice. AIDS patients: champagne, caviar, tango records: they'd *love* him!'

May couldn't fathom how any warm-blooded being tolerated a week of such cold, not to mention a lifetime, and she happily fled Peter's unwelcoming apartment for the warmer environs of the suburbs. For the McNellis house offered, at least, activity. It had more closets. And although June's cancer had proven itself a veritable black hole for attention and conversation and fuss, in all clouds a lining can be found. An example: no one jewed around with the damn thermostat anymore. The furnace was rattling and wheezing like it might blow, taking the whole superior McNellis family with it, straight to Cloud Nine. But the house was warm. May rubbed and rubbed her hands but no color came back. She peered out the train window and saw peeling slum windows with vacant interiors. The coloreds certainly couldn't take it, had hot-footed it, or cold-footed it, probably down to her town. Although, May thought, a little damn glass in the windows wouldn't have hurt.

The visit to Peter had been, as always, unsuccessful. Susan had been late to meet the train and May was forced to skitter around Grand Central's drunken maniacs. Peter had ignored the snapshots of his father, plucked with such hazard from the McNellises' picture box. His rejection had nearly ruined the Christmas dinner, or the so-called Christmas dinner: one skinny duck for three people surrounded by several tons of undercooked zucchini. There was, of course, no dessert. 'I had a wonderful plum pudding,' May lied. 'But I forgot it and Holly and Simon and Marilyn are probably lappin it up this very moment.' Susan replied, 'Would you like a banana?' The next day Peter claimed he had work. Susan fiddled around the kitchen, accepting May's intrusions with heavy patience and, by four o'clock, eyelids that actually fluttered at her. May decided to take a stroll, which lasted about four frigid minutes. She had hoped to be taken to a show. Instead, Susan produced an Indian dinner from five crusted pots. '*Wonderful*,' May said. 'It's *spreadin*!' They inquired earnestly about Simon's Indian cooking and May replied, 'The smells were *wonderful*. But everything came out brown.' The food was served: brown, laced with chili

and, amazingly, all vegetables. 'For health,' Peter stated.
May strained to reply: 'For niggers.' She picked at the
food with small, suspicious stabs. 'Isn't this *okra*?' May
attempted to divert the topic in a meaningful direction but
neither Peter nor Susan seemed interested in tales of Babe's
macrobiotic, cancer-conquering diet, which had, admit-
tedly, been a let-down, not leastways in taste. Peter droned
on about the Middle East. The Middle East! At Christmas!

She looked about the train compartment but no one
met her eager gaze. A greasy-haired Japanese sipped beer
across from her. He spasmed in a belch. The train went
through a tunnel and May shot a glance to the window-
turned-mirror. The eyes looked fine. She twisted up the
hair at her ears. May said to the Japanese man, 'Do you
know English? Even a little word or two?' Her stop came
quickly. No one was at the station to meet her, despite
her collect call from Grand Central. She stood on the
platform and bit her small, cold hand. An involuntary
whimper just slipped out. She looked about to see if
anyone had heard. But the people nearby were just
Japanese. Then, luckily, June's car pulled up to the platform and Simon honked.

'I drove Adrian to the airport,' Simon said, 'and stopped
at Jerry's.' He patted a small paper bag. 'There's a surprise
for you at home, May. A big surprise.'

May looked at him with astonished eyes.

'Just wait,' Simon said.

Warmth finally came to May. After years of shoddy
treatment the McNellises had come around, and not a
moment too soon, considering. Out of the three million
gay packages under the McNellis Christmas tree, shock-
ingly few had been hers. Her gifts must have been delayed
by UPS. May herself had ordered things by catalogue and
they never, ever came in time. Refunds were even slower.
It occurred to May that she was extremely fortunate: had
the presents been delayed just one more day, she would

73

have already departed and June would have distributed them among her pampered brats. But she tried to banish such negative thoughts. The image in May's mind of the McNellis Christmas tree wavered, altered and resolved into the Christmas tree of her youth, slightly stunted and strung with popcorn. She recalled a certain doll that had made one Christmas close to tolerable. The doll had real hair. Simon was humming gently and tapping the steering wheel: a woodpecker finding fine food in the grass. May also started to hum. 'Don't you love soul music, darlin? It makes me so happy the coloreds have somethin goin for them.'

'Blacks,' said Simon.

'Aren't they ever,' said May.

She scooted into the McNellis house and shot a glance under the Christmas tree. She could still see that doll, whose real hair May had finally hacked with scissors. The base of the McNellis tree was empty. Even the needles were gone: someone had vacuumed.

June McNellis stood at the dining-room table with her cane atilt. 'Look at me,' she crowed. 'I'm back from the dead!'

May stood tentatively in the living-room. She put her handbag down slowly. 'Back from the *dead*, darlin? *Why?*'

Holly described the new medication. 'Coughlin gave us the prescription Thursday. It's a miracle.' Simon showed it to May: a tiny, blue pill on his palm. 'That's a steroid,' he said.

May wanted to scream. 'It's the last thing I expected to find,' she said. 'And it's *wonderful*.'

'Of course, this isn't the best news,' June said.

May's eyes widened hopefully.

'They've canceled the second round of chemo. The ballgame is, in a way, over. That's why the steroids can be used. But I feel wonderful. I can eat again. I can walk. Look at my plate.' May saw the crusts of one of June's

74

damned sandwiches, which had once made her so fat. 'My first in weeks!'

'We were up till ten-thirty last night,' Simon called. He came to the table with a sandwich on a plate and started to eat. May looked at the sandwich. It was from Jerry's: the cause of her anguished minutes on the cold railway platform. She sat on the edge of one of the dining-room chairs. 'That's so *wonderful*, darlin.' Her pale hands danced closer and closer to June. 'We had the *best* time at Peter's place. He is *so* lonely without Babe.'

May looked at Simon's sandwich. She was ravenous. 'Is that wonderful, darlin? It looks *wonderful*.'

'When we went to Japan, Don and I were going to bring a Jerry's sausage-and-pepper sandwich.' June's tone had been transformed. The sick woman was thoroughly exorcised. 'But we thought it would go bad.'

'They brought corned-beef hash instead. I'll never forget that first night. Unloading all those cans of corned-beef hash.'

'I remember every moment of that trip.'

'So do I, Mom.'

'Susan and Peter brought me to a show last evening,' May said. 'And it was wonderful! And Peter just *loved* the pictures of his father from the picture box. Those duplicates.' Which, in fact, were still scrambled at the bottom of May's commodious handbag. But no one paid attention or even asked the show. The black hole had, amazingly, increased its gravitational pull. And the McNellises were no fans of the city. The only one who ever got there was Marilyn, on distinctly dirty-sounding dates.

Then came the damn naps. May paced the house, pulled laundry from the basement and threw it on the dining-room table in case anyone came in. She watched television and smoked a succession of cigarettes. The evening was long – June's steroids had boosted both appetite *and* thirst

75

– with only one interesting moment. Simon referred to a 'short-ball' colleague. May leapt at the opportunity.

'Why darlin, is penis size *really* so important to men?'

'I guess so.'

'Well I've only seen five penises in my life. Six including Babe. And I don't know, they seemed pretty much alike to me. Kinda like, I don't know, Japanese cars.'

Everyone at the table was silent, evaluating May's enumeration of the penises in her life. 'I mean, what's normal?'

'I guess six to eight inches,' said Simon.

'Like this darlin? Or like this?'

'That's the range.'

Then May told a not entirely true story about a friend of hers named Earl and a vacation in which it was only natural the two of them share a room because they weren't but sleepin a few hours. And how he came back from the bathroom with just a towel around his neck. And his penis was the tiniest little thing she had ever seen, no bigger than this. And she didn't know *what* to do.

'Was it erect?' asked Simon clinically.

'Of course darlin. It was just stickin straight out as proud as can be.'

'That *is* small.'

It was a good story and May felt briefly regarded, even though she had never seen Earl's damn penis, never particularly desired to, but always suspected him of having a short one when he showed so little interest after Babe died. And, of course, she had seen him at the pool a few times, and you can kinda tell when the man scratches himself. As all men do. Especially with those Spandex type suits.

Simon embarked on a long story about Hong Kong and May excused herself. She darted up the stairs for a quick reconnaissance of his room. She darted through Simon's door into the long attic closet. Her white doll's hand grasped the neck of a stately cologne bottle. She whisked it downstairs, dumped the sour liquid in the bathroom sink and placed the bottle under a skirt in her suitcase. When she returned to the dining-room everyone was laughing and she said, 'What's that darlin?' She stared directly at Simon, her eyes just as open and innocent as they could be.

May waited them all out, her face directed toward the television screen, cigarette after cigarette lit and extinguished. She thought of June's illness and the little blue pills. The idea of June's demise came closer to home. May thought of Ruthie and her money and realized it was nothing but the dregs of the McNellis family. Her dregs. The television flickered, washing its liquid light over May's frozen expression. Her ash grew perilously long. When the house was finally quiet, or as quiet as it got these days with June's radio, May stood and started her long night's quest. In the basement, a noise made her jump to her feet, her pale hands at her face. Her expression: one of utter innocence. But it was just a house noise. The same thing happened in the attic, which she reached through the girls' room, penetrating the section that was just beyond Simon's chest of inset drawers. She had looked for peep-holes around the drawers but found none. The noise made her freeze; she waited for discovery and none came; then she began anew. When she had finished for the night and was shutting June's china closet, her attention was drawn to the large needlepoint on the dining-room wall. It was Ruthie's. May had nearly forgotten it. She noted it in her mind and, arms filled, retired silently to her room, nicely tuckered out.

The next day, May rolled her enormous suitcase into the front hall. 'I had to leave Daniel's starter set in the closet,' she said. 'I just didn't have the room in this damn bag. I'll get it next time.' She smoked a final cigarette at the table, waiting for Kevin to arrive. June was talking animatedly, high on her little blue steroids. Simon and Holly were in the kitchen, starting lunch preparations.

'Shhh!' Holly held up her hand. 'Listen.'

May's voice came from the dining-room. ' . . . the darlin mentioned it to me at the nursing home and she was so pathetic. It was one of her moods, you know. She said she wanted it for that ugly blank wall in her kitchen. You know that wall, June?'

'She's after the needlepoint,' Holly hissed. 'I've wanted that needlepoint for years and Mom said I could have it. She's trying to get in with Ruthie.'

The melodious, slow voice – May's only languorous feature – continued. 'Ruthie has such fond memories of it, you know. Maurice inherited it from his grandmother. And I *know* I have a lot of luggage, darlin, but . . . '

Simon put his finger to his lips. 'Wait.' Finally they heard June's voice, firm and dismissing. The needlepoint was saved.

Holly whispered, 'I'm so goddamned mad.'

Before she left, May suggested dates for her next visit. June cut her off. 'Let's not make any plans.' Her voice was weary. 'Let's take it day to day.'

That afternoon, as Simon and June talked at the table, Holly sat herself on the carpet before the china closet. She exclaimed, 'Uh-oh.' Simon and June looked at her.

'I know this closet inside out. If you don't put everything back in its right place, the whole thing gets screwed up.'

'That's true,' said June. 'It's always been that way.'

'*Someone's* been going through this closet.' Holly's movements became more agitated. 'There was another cup here. You know my tea cups, Mom? The mismatched ones? I'm sure I had . . . ' Her eyes glittered with fury. She squatted to penetrate more deeply into the closet.

'No one would steal a tea cup, Holly. Even May. What would she do with it?'

Holly took out all the tea cups, matching them with saucers. 'I *know* there were more. I'm sure of it. That bitch took them. She's been stealing our china.'

'Let's look on this side.' Simon squatted at the adjacent door. 'Maybe they were misplaced after Christmas.'

'It wouldn't surprise me in the least.' June exhaled blue cigarette smoke. 'And I'm telling you both, listen to me, at the funeral you have to watch that woman.'

'My God,' said Simon. 'She'll be here for the funeral.'

'Of course,' said June. 'You'll have no choice. The first thing to hide is your grandmother's silver. Including the dishes and those napkin rings on the bookshelf. May adores silver.'

'I can't believe this,' said Holly. 'I'm so goddamned mad.'

June puffed again. 'And watch my wedding photos. May asked about them yesterday. She said she wanted to see Babe. She's got her eyes on them.'

Days passed and, on a morning of bitter cold, Simon left. The greenhouse windows were crystallized and the furnace screamed as never before. June said, 'You better invest in a new one if the house is sold. What's six or seven thousand dollars?' The steroids continued to buoy her and Simon said over coffee, 'I really hate to go, Mom. I'm going to miss your great days.' A honk sounded from the driveway. Simon turned his attention to his bags. He kissed June lightly on the cheek and carried his suitcase out of the house. The taxi driver, wearing a black sweatshirt with a hood, said, 'Fuckin early. Fuckin *cold.*' Simon had waved from the driveway tens of times before, always aware of the portentous quality of such goodbyes. But this time the portentousness wasn't imagined. He looked to the doorway and saw his mother standing erect, proud, illness barely reflected in her slimness. She wore the navy-blue cardigan over watchplaid slacks and a white blouse, collar raised in the rear. One hand grasped the ugly steel cane. She waved the other arm in a wide arc above her head. She continued to stand there, ignoring the cold. The arm moved slowly, from right to left, over and over. A burning cigarette showed in the hand. Simon realized his mother's message: *Just in case, Simon, I will say goodbye.* The driver fumbled with a clipboard. June waved, regular and slow, the red door with its wreath visible behind

her. The car rolled down the driveway past the supine
Christmas tree on the curbside, dirty tinsel glinting in the
frozen lawn. June adjusted the cane and waved again.
Simon saw the cold entering the open door behind her,
chilling the living-room, the dining-room, the greenhouse
in turn, pouring down the circular staircase to surround
the screaming furnace in the cellar. It poured into the
house in the other direction: down the hall, into the den,
sweeping out the fetid air of his mother's sickroom. It
travelled up the staircase, chilling equally the two bedrooms until it converged, via the twin louvered doors, in
the frosty attic closet. Simon felt the whole house growing
cold, its frame heaving in a massive skeletal shiver: a house
noise to end all house noises. He gave a weak, final wave.
June diminished and disappeared as the taxi turned at
Vera Sherman's house and sped toward the thruway.

The flights were long; one was delayed. Simon looked
through the plane's window at the distant, unshadowed
tundra. He was obsessed with the image of June McNellis
in the doorway, giving that brave, deliberate gesture.
Simon found himself unsure and upset. That mechanical
wave; that jaunty stance, defiant cigarette in hand; the
enigmatic smile. Was the gesture so unambiguous: that of
a fast-cooling sun beckoning farewell to its satellites? He
saw the old woman, the house engulfing her, the cold air
pouring unimpeded around her. Was it a simple goodbye?
Couldn't the gesture be seen as a warning? A last-minute
change of mind? Couldn't June McNellis have been telling
Simon: break free!

January

A blue ribbon of smoke floated through paler mist. A red coal flared in the dark. A desperate, ragged voice echoed from a dream: 'I've had it all! Am I too late . . . I've had it all . . . Can't I pass it on? . . . '

Simon McNellis was wrapped in a rough wool blanket with rubbery, fingerlike fringe. From the terrace he waited for the sky to lighten above the neighboring houses. The morning sounds of India would soon begin: the vast, sloppy family rising from its rumpled bed. He had preceded it by hours. A blow-heater did its best at his feet, pushing insistent wintertime mist around the terrace's cement pots. Simon's hand drooped; a long ash fell from a firm American cigarette. A single word snaked through his thoughts, tying them together and then tearing them apart.

We had a good Christmas, considering.

We're holding up.

We.

The sounds of morning built. Ramesh would be the first up. He'd make milky, sugary tea laced with cardamom and bring it to Simon on a lacquer tray bought by June McNellis in Nikko, now scarred with use.

Simon had been home more than a week. Each morning or evening the phone rang with an update from Holly. On two occasions, June got on the line, vibrant and cheery. Simon's return date was not fixed but everyone knew it would come soon: perhaps after the next phone call. By fleeing to the other side of the world, he had escaped the illness and the numbing anti-routine of the sick house. But a contagion had already infected him and, in the Indian atmosphere, it flourished.

We McNellises. When his father had died, the family had simply shrunk a notch. Why wasn't it the same now?

Ramesh, small and skinny as a girl, pushed through the scuffed white door at the top of the stairs. He scanned the terrace with the look of a scared bird. 'Morn sah'b!' His voice was high and timid. Simon gestured absently from the chaise-longue.

Ramesh emerged from the kitchen with the tea on the tray. Simon was stretched on the chaise, boyishness incarnate, cigarette incinerating in his hand. He accepted the tea. When his eyes met Ramesh's, they showed no life, or no nearby life. Ramesh scurried away.

The day had begun. The cook ambled in, followed by the sweeper. All paid respect to the thin master on the chaise-longue. Strangers looked down on Simon from neighboring buildings: fat people on balconies with smug tea cups, thin, sharp-eyed servants on rooftops bearing laundry and baskets. From one house a Doberman panted hungrily. India was all eyes at all times. But Simon didn't notice or didn't care.

Priscilla arrived on the terrace, hair wet and combed, en route to the High Commission. She wore her grandmother's brooch. 'This has to be the longest jetlag in history,' she complained. Later, the dhobi panted up the stairs and the driver came up to collect the car keys.

The spell was broken. Simon moved among the rooms of the apartment, barefoot in draw-string pants, waiting for its return.

At dusk, the procession reversed itself. The mist held off until after nine and then blanketed the rooftops, effac-

ing the broad Indian sky and the stars and planets behind
it. Priscilla went to bed early. Ramesh piled coal on a
brazier before he retired. Simon resumed his place on the
chaise. He adjusted the rough blanket. He looked at his
torso, washed by milky, inconstant light and was
reminded anew of his mother on Christmas night watching
her children by similar flickers from the greenhouse television. June's face had been in shadow.

We.

We know what June McNellis saw that night: her three
children grown large, handsome, ostensibly complete.
Scattered but not strayed. Time's blemishes erased. In the
aquarium lighting of the greenhouse, Simon had twitched
his adolescent hips. Marilyn teenybopped. Holly sang in
the heartbreaking voice of a schoolgirl. But what June
McNellis saw would never be known precisely. How she
saw *us*: what we were, are, will be. That small, once-
vital solar system – the perfect McNellises – now facing
obliteration.

For they had been a solar system unto its own: tilted
away from the town and rising slightly above. Money,
June said, wasn't everything, thank Christ. Class was
something other people either didn't have or didn't use
properly. Irishness set them apart from the main and gave
them the insider's laugh over fellow Irish. The local church
was as needy of the McNellises as the reverse. It was June,
not Don, who spun these insistent, sacred threads and
they hardened over the years into cables: flexible but firm,
of different lengths for each of the satellites. They
restrained – no one understood more than Simon – but
they also fixed the McNellises in individual, permanent
orbits.

Simon wondered: is it *we* McNellises? Or was it always
me? And what happens to us when that central *me* dis-
appears?

Simon lit another cigarette, thinking back to the death

of his father. A movement on a rooftop distracted him. A silhouette of a woman in a sari beckoned urgently in the opposite direction. That house had been a mere skeleton two years earlier, a charcoal sketch in brick against the cobalt sky. His mother had examined it and said, 'It's like a Lego house.' Each evening, as the two of them sat on the terrace, a bamboo flute played the sad song of an off-duty construction worker far from his home village. A horn honked on the street below. The woman in the sari, the lovely shade, disappeared and the rooftop was again square and dull. But once it had produced music. June and Simon had sat drinking tall bottles of beer. They had battled for the second time of their lives. Simon, this time, had won. They had been to each other what they had always been. They had talked and talked, outlasting the entire neighborhood, the entire sleepy subcontinent. They froze the night with their talk, which only the powerful Indian dawn was able to thaw.

On one of those nights, his mother told a story no other McNellis would ever hear. It was a story she wouldn't have told without the intimate Indian night, the soulful throb of the bamboo flute, the vast distance between India and that house on the hill.

The guards in their turbans had drifted off to sleep. Traffic had expired. Puddles from the beer bottles threatened June's purchases, which were spread on the glass-topped table: big eggs of brass, gay papier-maché boxes, two tiny silver boxes with a red gem in each. Long silences punctuated each flute raga; each seemed the last. June told her story set in the house on the hill, in the back bedroom overlooking the garden and the tall fence hiding the rumbling thruway. It was night. June and Don, wife and husband, lay together in their bed for the final time. The diagnosis was confirmed. Don would check into the hospital the following morning for the surgery that would kill him. He lay in the bed frozen with fear. June moved

88

slowly toward the center of the bed until her back nestled against her husband's side. Don failed to react. The bedroom lights were out, erasing the yellow rectangles visible from Vera Sherman's house. The couple lay there, unmoving, until Don finally shifted, arose, dressed and left the house. June remained still, listening to the sound of the departing car. Some hours later, Don returned and went back to bed. But it was morning and June got up. She cooked breakfast and drove him to the hospital.

Simon asked again and again: Why? What does it mean? June said she didn't know. Where did he go? June had no idea. But . . . ? She wouldn't even guess.

We? What are we, Simon wondered. Can a family be an extension of one parent alone? For the McNellises had recovered from Don's death. The existing order was shaken but eventually restored. On those Indian nights, Simon watched his mother force it back into balance. She let loose great chunks of herself to accomplish it. It was unlike anything in the family's history and anything in June's past behavior. Out flew the massive chunks, churning the tides. Ugly stretches of sea floor were exposed. The battle between June and Simon over the McNellis house was the climactic tidal wave. And balance was regained, order restored. The tide covered the ugly mud, never to ebb so low again. The damage was slight, the system merely reduced, the radiuses pulled tighter.

And now, the very sun cooled. In Simon's dream, it exploded. Darkness had fallen, cold descended and violent pleas ricocheted through the endless dark of sleep, pleas cried over and over in a distinct, ravaged voice: 'I've had it all! Can't you take it? Can't I pass it on?' There were unruly clouds, tinged sickly white, with a throbbing hole in the center. 'Are none of you worthy of me? I've had it all! Am I too late? Can't you take it . . . ' That's when Simon awoke, Priscilla groaned and he gathered his blankets for the chaise on the blackened terrace.

February

From the airport, Simon was again struck by the dented grayness of the city, that dead high-rise machine. India was rotten but alive: young, crawling, the color of a mature bruise. New York was a rusted sign, swinging slowly, destined to fall on a dead pavement. Then he was pulled away and the neat winter suburbs, skinny houses in steel-colored groves, swung into view. He spotted the fence above the thruway and said to no one, 'That's my house.' The limo exited and wended through slim, bare trees. At Vera Sherman's, Simon said, 'Right.' In the driveway he said, 'Could you honk the horn. Once more. They couldn't hear.'

Simon made his way up the walk. In the doorway, Holly and Marilyn Beth stood shoulder to shoulder. He quickly kissed each sister. Holly put a hand on his arm. 'She's waiting.' In his overcoat, Simon walked to the rear bedroom to find June smiling up from bed, adjusting her pillow. She fumbled with the blaring radio. 'Hi honey.' Her eyes glittered from layers of monstrously swollen flesh. Simon recognized the corpse he had stumbled across in a sweltering cane field in Mindanao. 'We've been waiting so long.' June touched her face. 'This will go down. It's only when I lie in bed.'

In the living-room, Simon gestured at the famous pink portrait. 'It's unbelievable!' The phone rang.

'Hello Mrs Sherman. I don't know *what* time I'm on. Yes, Holly says the swelling is improved, since the radiation. But if that's an improvement . . . '

Marilyn Beth called from the living-room, 'I've got Spanish!' The door slammed. Simon opened the refrigerator expecting to find his usual favorites. But it was empty. In the back, near the breadcrumbs, was a paper packet from Christmas containing two curled pieces of green salami. He got beer from the garage and put it in the freezer.

'Where did that come from?' An enlarged photo of Simon floated in a huge lucite frame in the living-room.

'I found the frame after Christmas.' Holly said. 'Mom was looking at the picture.'

'I don't know if I'll enjoy staring at my soulful self all day. I thought Mom didn't like that picture.'

'She said your skin looked rough. Somehow that doesn't bother her anymore.'

'She looks godawful.'

'Yes,' said Holly. 'She does, doesn't she? We forget. The radiation *has* helped. Wait till you see her sitting up. Her face almost gets back to normal.'

Simon carried his suitcase to the stairs and paused. He walked back to the living-room. 'I think I'll stay in the den this time. Closer to Mom.' He deposited the suitcase and used the bathroom. He brought his face close to the mirror. In the living-room, he picked up the photo.

'Is this really prominent?' He turned his head and pointed at a blemish on his left cheek.

'Simon, don't be silly. I had never noticed it.'

'Until the photo.'

'Well, yes.'

Simon returned the frame to the coffee table. He turned it away from the dining-room.

'Listen Simon. Kevin and I have decided. About the

94

house. We *are* going to take it! If we can afford it, of course. But the emotional decision is made.'

'Great.' Simon opened a can of beer.

'It's always been clear in my mind. But I was worried about Kevin. I thought he didn't want to live in Mom and Dad's house. But it was the opposite. He really wants to. It's such a relief. I've *always* wanted this house.' The far wall thumped; the gilded mirror trembled. 'Oh shit, I forgot her Saltines.'

When she returned, Holly said, 'Mom wants you to learn the security system. So you can arm it at night. And when you go out.'

'Swelling of the face. Paranoia. Any other symptoms I should know about?'

'Constipation?'

'Sorry I asked.'

The security system was controlled by a small plastic pad near the front door. It had blinking green lights and numerals. Holly taught him the codes.

'Remember, you have two minutes after you've opened the door. Then the siren blows. And believe me, you don't want that. They can hear it in Manhattan.'

'1 – 9 – 3 – 1. How can I remember that?'

'It's the year Babe was born. *Darlin*.'

'Isn't that just *wonderful*! How the hell do I know when Babe was born?'

'I'll bring Mom out. It's time. We have to wheel her these days.'

June glided through the house in the chair with the huge plastic wheels. At the table, she slowly smoothed her hair. 'Get me that mirror, honey.' She looked at her swollen face. 'Just wait a few minutes. You'll see the difference.' Her eyes were terrifying: sparkling, frightened marbles behind lids of death-colored flesh. Simon half-feared a commensurate change within. 'And get those curtains, honey. And the drapes.'

Holly said goodbye and Simon ordered a pizza over the phone. June's face started to recede. Every few minutes, she checked the silver hand-mirror. At the end, the slight puffiness gave an illusion of health, as if June's unmourned menopausal pounds had returned. She fumbled clumsily with a button on her blue satin nightgown: she no longer dressed to come out of the bedroom. Simon noticed stains. The satin between the buttons gaped, revealing a deflated breast, a gray stomach.

'What on earth is that?'

'Pretty, isn't it?' June's chest and neck were covered in blood-red slashes. 'From the radiation.' The radiologist painted her to facilitate the daily placement of his machines. He didn't care that his marks disfigured the patient: if she lived, the marks would eventually fade. If the patient died, which was more common, the undertaker had seen worse.

June accepted a Bloody Mary. The phone rang. 'No, I'm not in Japan anymore,' said Simon. 'I left many years ago. Yes, they visited me . . . yes, they both loved it . . . yes, I'm sure Daddy showed you the pictures. He showed everybody.'

June ate half a slice of pizza. 'I want to decide the big things now,' she said, 'so there'll be no fighting later. Marilyn Beth, as you know, wants Grandma's ring.' She fingered the diamond on her left hand. 'Holly can have my engagement ring. That leaves you.' Simon chose an heirloom. 'And, of course, Marilyn also wants my big gold bracelet.' In this way, they distributed china, silver, the crystal candlesticks, two good paintings and the dining-room table, which Holly and Kevin wanted.

'Your portrait, Mom.' Simon gestured at the front wall. Between the front windows, curtains pulled fearfully, young June McNellis flexed her perfect chin to the ceiling.

'I always loved it but what would you kids do with it?

96

Where would anyone put a dead mother's portrait? On the stairwell, I guess, like in *Rebecca*.'

'My driver would take it,' Simon said. 'He'd build a shrine.'

'Ram . . . what's his name?'

'Ramakrishnan.' Priscilla had informed the servants about June's illness. For days, they nodded gravely at Simon, eyes flashing with dark awe. On the drive to the airport, as the car sped through the misty Indian night, Ramakrishnan had paid his respects to June. Simon thanked him. Ramakrishnan said, 'She gave me life. I think her god.'

June's eyes grew wide with wonder. 'What on earth?'

'Remember when we returned from Agra? And Ramakrishnan came down with typhoid?'

'Of course I remember. He was shaking like a dog. It was the water in Agra. That's what he said.'

'And you put him on the verandah chair and wrapped him in that blanket. And we sent out for the pills?'

'I remember . . . '

'Apparently, this episode has evolved in Ramakrishnan's mind. You saved his life. You are a minor Indian goddess.' Simon said he'd erect a shrine on a country roadside with thick, salmon-painted mud walls. The interior would be dominated by the pink portrait of June McNellis flexing her chin toward the Hindu heaven. 'By the next century, you could be worshipped by several million people. Of course, you'll have to come through with a miracle or two.'

'That shouldn't be hard. In India.'

'You better bring your checkbook.'

'I have a feeling Marilyn Beth has her eyes on that already. *And* my Citicard.'

The house had remained the same: not the house of Simon's childhood, although the cracked Rex Stouts still saluted from the upstairs bookshelf and the forlorn coats awaited inspection in the attic closet. It was the house he encountered first at Christmastime. Its routines were disrupted, its calm permanently hectored by June's shouting radio. The only noises to overcome it were the house's shocking starts – grown louder with the fallen temperature – and the anguished groans of the furnace, piped everywhere through grills thick with decades of white paint. Simon shut the den door and pulled out the sofa-bed. He lay in bed, looking at the unfamiliar white blinds and listening to the house's uneasy sounds. He concluded: 'Holly and Kevin, you can have it.'

The idea of a party was inappropriate, of course, beneath bad taste, ludicrous. But the steroids' magic continued and the McNellises acknowledged their over-zealousness in closing ranks: too many of June's well-wishers had been barred from the house on the hill. So Holly and Simon decided on a one-shot occasion with Indian food. A familiar excitement swept the house. The McNellises had always punctuated their lives with parties. June saw nothing untoward about the idea. 'But we're having no party,' she warned, 'until those back drapes are hemmed.'

Adrian's reaction, over the cordless telephone, was predictable.

'Yes, Adrian.' Simon nodded at his mother, who sat in the wheelchair picking polish off her nails. 'You bring the champagne. And yes, of course, the Jitterbug records.'

'I always hated the Jitterbug.' June brushed pink flakes from her lap. 'And the Continental.'

Then Adrian pulled a surprise. He insisted on bringing Ruthie from the nursing home. June protested weakly. Vera Sherman offered her spare room, which Simon thought a good idea.

'We'll say I have to stay in the den, Mom. Ruthie can't make the stairs. We'll barely see her.'

'All right,' said June. 'But no May.'

99

Holly spoke with unusual firmness. 'No, Mom, no May.'

'Poor Vera.' June looked out the back window, puffing on a Carlton. 'She'll walk through her living-room with an armload of laundry and Ruthie, in that voice, will say: "Got a match?" I can't count how many times she said that. "Got a match?" I thought Don would kill her.'

Adrian arrived in the evening in his Irish hat, guiding Ruthie slowly up the walk. She had shrunk or, more accurately, receded into a medium-sized hump on her back. Her woolly head bobbed at the level of Simon's chest; of her face only a trembling, curled lip was visible. He asked how the nursing home was. Ruthie muttered, *'Deplorable!'*

In the kitchen, in his terrible stage whisper, Adrian described the trip up.

'I was determined to get one positive word out of her. She was not impressed by the train or the meal and she was right about the meal, it was appalling. Finally when the sun set she had to admit it was pretty. Better, she said, than the sunsets at the nursing home.

Simon and Holly debated the chili level of the Indian dishes. Holly pleaded restraint and Simon defended authenticity. 'Okay,' Simon conceded, 'I'll make the chickpeas hot. No one will eat them anyway.'

'I mean, a little hotness is okay . . . '

'Try this.' Simon shoved a spoon at Holly's mouth.

Adrian happily volunteered to collect Grace at the train station. He lost frantic minutes searching for his hat.

'I know that look,' Holly said. 'Better watch her.'

'I know Grace,' said Simon. 'Don't worry.'

They looked up. Vera Sherman was grinning in the doorway in a peach-colored dress. 'Here's a salad.' She placed it on the kitchen counter. She whispered, 'Ruthie's settled, but she's none too happy.'

'Want to go see Mom, Mrs Sherman? Come on Simon.'

They found June lying on her back, rubber eyelids aimed at the ceiling.

'Mom?'

'I hear you.'

'Mrs Sherman's here, Mom.' June turned her balloon head, adjusting the pillow.

'Hello Vera. Isn't this swelling incredible? I feel like my face is going to burst.'

Vera Sherman stood in the doorway with her hands folded. She didn't bat an eye. 'I thought the radiation helped, June.'

'I guess. But the sensation. I can't describe.'

'We're going to get you up now, Mom,' said Simon, 'so the swelling can go down.' His voice dropped. 'Ruthie's here.'

'I heard,' June said.

'She's crabby as ever,' Vera said.

'Okay guys.' With a blind motion, June threw off the comforter. 'It's time, I guess.' The satin nightgown was hiked to her hips. Stick legs floundered on the bed. Simon turned from the sight of her uncovered groin.

When he returned to the living-room, he found a lively group. Fred McNellis, Don's older brother, sipped Scotch with dark concentration and unsteady hands. Adrian appeared in the kitchen doorway, uncorking a bottle of wine and shouting a story in the direction of the dining-room. Ruthie was sunk in the wing chair, rattling ice in a heavy rum sour. There was a cracking sound, a twitch of the curled lip. Ruthie chewed her ice.

Rhonda, Fred's wife, sat next to Grace on the love seat. She was frantically whispering in Grace's ear. Grace looked toward Simon, eyes widened in silent appeal. Rhonda jumped up and rushed to Simon. 'Don't worry dear,' she whispered fiercely, 'I'm driving!' Then she bee-lined for Fred, who was booming to no one in particular, 'That's what I told the Cardinal!' Fred was shorter than

Don had been, utterly orange in complexion and densely built. His face was Don's except for his features, which crowded nervously around his nose. He spoke in a loud, exasperated boom. '*I* told him. But did it do any *good*?'

Simon took Rhonda's place on the love seat. Grace patted his knee and sighed. Then she put a finger in her ear as if to swab it out. 'Her nose. It actually went in my ear!'

'Rhonda's a big whisperer.'

'I don't think I've *ever*.' Grace gave Simon a formal hug hello. 'And tell me please.' She blinked with exaggerated bewilderment. 'What is a *Twig*?'

Fred's voice continued to boom through the living-room. Rhonda's stiff, flaming red hair shook fondly. She extended an arm around her husband's ample back.

Marilyn Beth bustled through the front door and went straight for Ruthie in the wing chair. She squatted, spoke, listened and rose, rolling her eyes at Simon and Grace. She said buoyantly, 'I need a beer. Ready for a refill, Ruthie?' A smudged and empty glass lunged from the wing chair, grasped in a shaky, crabbed hand.

Simon went to answer the doorbell. He was engulfed in a brown, woolly bear-hug lasting a full minute. Two pudgy hands kneaded his cheeks: he looked down into watery, pale eyes. 'How is Mom? I only heard last week!' The accent was European, only slightly diminished from his boyhood. He grasped the woman's hand and led her to the dining-room. 'This is Gerta,' he announced.

'Where's Mom?' Gerta was small and stocky. She looked at Grace with teary blue eyes. 'I've known June since they were like this.' She pushed down Simon's shoulder. 'I only heard last week. From Vera. She said it was . . .' – Gerta looked around the room and over her shoulder – '*cancer*. I have cake in the car. But where is Mom? Where is she?'

'Holly's bringing her out soon. You remember Adrian, Gerta.'

Gerta hugged Adrian distractedly. 'We used to sell the milk together at Assumption. Where is she?'

There was a deep rumble and everyone looked up. Holly pushed the horrible wheelchair. June wore the blue silk dress, which didn't quite cover the red slashes on her neck. Her hair was combed, her face only slightly puffy. She smiled and gave a casual wave. 'Hello Gerta. Hello Grace. It's so nice to see you.'

Simon heard Gerta gasp. She looked up at him, tears washing her milky eyes. A handkerchief flew to Gerta's face.

The wheelchair paused in front of Ruthie's chair.

'How are you, Ruthie?' asked June.

'Been better, June.'

'So have I.'

'Haven't we all,' said Holly, wheeling June the final distance to her place at the table. From the kitchen came a popping sound. Adrian emerged, followed by Fred and Rhonda, with a foaming bottle of champagne.

'Where's Judge Houlihan? I'm sure he was invited! This is his cure for cancer!' Holly got champagne glasses from the china closet.

Rhonda rushed to June and whispered in her ear. Fred boomed at Marilyn Beth: 'The original system was perfectly fine. It was a little old. It was a little unglamorous. But it worked! And then they went and screwed it up! Not that I blame the President.'

At the table, there was an illusion of normality, despite the black wheelchair. Simon collected extra chairs. Holly helped Ruthie to the table, seating her next to Grace.

'Where's Caroline?'

'Where do you think she is, Mom?' asked Holly. 'She'll be here sooner or later.'

'I want to show you all something,' June announced. 'Simon? I think it's time.'

Simon went to the kitchen. He returned with a tall glass of water in one hand, the other extended like an offering. 'That,' he said, 'is a steroid.'

'I recommend them,' said June, 'to everyone.' She put the blue pill into her mouth and drank the water in slow, clumsy gulps.

Gerta's eyes flooded with fresh tears.

The conversation shifted to the old days when June and Gerta worked at the Assumption Mothers Guild.

'What was her name June? They lived in that big, yellow house . . . '

'Lydia Witt.'

'Lydia.' Gerta pronounced the name slowly, awkwardly, her accent going back twenty years with the memory.

June stubbed out a cigarette. 'She was the one who always said: "Where are *we* going? *We* aren't finished." And I said, "*We* are finished because *we* have a child at home waiting for *we*." She was the only person I ever told off. Ross had to give me a tranquilizer to do it. Remember, Vera?'

Vera nodded. 'You were shaking! So was I!'

'It was one of the best things I ever did in my life.' June lit a new cigarette, triumph on her face. 'It was the only tranquilizer I ever took in my life!'

'Whatever happened to Mrs Witt?' asked Simon.

'The daughter had that car crash,' said Vera. 'What was her name?'

'Angelica,' said Marilyn Beth. 'She was in my class.'

'Paralyzed.' Vera put her hand at her collar-bone and moved it downward. 'Ross saw her that night.'

'Then they moved,' said Gerta, wide-eyed. 'Divorced!'

Adrian's voice announced, 'There's something on the Middle East.' Rhonda and Fred followed him to the greenhouse. Fred's voice lingered behind: 'They're all like that, they're all *faglers* in the arts.'

Gerta talked about the final days of her late husband Ilya. 'Ilya thought we should take care of health, our health.' She became teary-eyed. 'So we started taking the vitamins. And then, right after that, I had kidney stone.' Gerta pressed her belly vigorously. 'It's so painful! And I told him: no more vitamins. These vitamins, I say, they're going to kill us!'

The phone rang. Holly listened for a second and then hung up. 'Caroline is on her way, Mom.'

'She was always late,' complained Ruthie. 'So was Babe. The two of them. Always late.'

'And then Ilya said we should stop eating the butter.' Gerta leaned emphatically across the table. 'For the cholesterol. So we stopped eating butter. Except in the cakes. And Ilya got these back pains.' She pressed her back. 'Tremendous back pains. He couldn't get out of bed.'

Ruthie went to the bathroom, aided by Marilyn Beth.

'And then,' Gerta continued, 'we started taking walks around the neighborhood. Just for exercise. And Ilya died.' Her eyes welled with tears and her soggy handkerchief flew to her blue eyes. 'I went to see him in the hospital and they said, *kaput!*'

The door pushed open. A youthful woman in a sequined tee-shirt strode into the room, rubbing her hands. She came straight to June's chair, flicked back long straight hair and kissed her on the forehead. She said, 'I couldn't get away, I tried to call a million times. June, you're looking just great.'

'This is Caroline, my sister-in-law,' said June. 'You've met Gerta, haven't you Caroline?'

'Years ago.' Caroline threw back her head and gave a full, wonderful laugh. 'Let's not count them!'

Simon whispered, 'Babe's first wife. Before May.

Darlin.' Grace took a long look. She raised an eyebrow at Simon and whispered, 'Aging bravely?'

'And this is Grace, Simon's friend.'

Grace got a half-handshake and then Caroline knelt to greet Ruthie. She nodded distractedly for several minutes. She stood, straightened her shirt and strode up to Adrian. 'Get me a drink, for God's sake.' She laughed a dismissing laugh. 'Never, never get into the travel business. Believe me!'

The party was now spread among the dining-room, the kitchen and greenhouse. Gerta rushed outside and returned with a perfect strudel. Adrian opened another bottle of champagne, invoking Judge Houlihan.

'What happened to the daughter?' asked Gerta. 'The retarded one?'

'Epileptic,' said Simon. '*She* was in my class.'

Gerta raised a twisted hand to her chest. 'I used to let her take the milk for free.'

'Rotten little brat,' said June. 'I used to tell her I'd cut off that hand if she stole another carton of milk.'

'How's India?' Caroline sipped a Bloody Mary.

'Backward,' said Simon. 'Very far away.'

'I bet,' she laughed, shaking her head dismissingly. 'I met the ambassador in Washington. Some kind of old Maharaja.' She wagged her head stupidly, popped her eyes and laughed again.

Grace delivered a fresh drink to Ruthie.

'I was going to move in here, when Doc was alive,' Ruthie said. 'But June got ruthless. Positively ruthless.'

Grace squatted clumsily next to Ruthie's chair. 'What do you mean ruthless?'

'June said Don died. But I never believed it. Then she had her plane crash. Big excusers, all of them.'

'Mrs McNellis had a plane crash?'

'Of course.' Ruthie swirled her glass. 'One of those trips

to, you know, Europe.' The gray lip sucked up an ice cube.

'You mean to Asia? To visit Simon?'

'No.' Ruthie gave a gray scowl. The ice cube cracked. 'To Europe. Italy and where's that place? Where Princess Grace lives? Monte Carlo?'

'Monaco.'

'That's it. That's why she's sick now. She was the only survivor. Princess Grace died.'

'Yes,' said Grace, 'she did.'

Ruthie nodded with quiet triumph and shook her drink. 'Served them right if you ask me. Though no one ever does.'

Grace stood, removed her glasses and rubbed her nose. She opened her eyes to find Fred staring at her redly. He pointed. 'I told them at your editorial page.' He shook his head skeptically. 'Did they *listen*?'

The Indian food was served. Caroline made knowing, appreciative sounds, scooping into all the dishes. Gerta picked with sharp, suspicious eyes. Rhonda filled Fred's plate several times. Ruthie ate everything on her plate, including an enormous portion of chickpeas. Everyone praised the strudel and Gerta became teary-eyed. She departed, hugging Simon tightly at the door. The cold air poured in. He could feel the warmth from the small, dense woman. She spoke of her grandchild. He walked her to the car and hugged her once more, grasping the strudel platter awkwardly over her shoulder.

When he returned, June had been wheeled to bed. Holly returned with an odd glow in her eyes.

'Mom says I should ask Ruthie about the needlepoint. I'm going to do it!'

Holly and Vera led Ruthie home. Adrian lured most of the group into the greenhouse for the newscast from the Middle East. In the kitchen, Simon found Caroline. He poured her a glass of wine and opened a fresh beer.

'So, Si-*mon*.' Caroline leaned back against the counter showing her slim, girlish shape. 'What's going to happen to the McNellises? Afterwards? If you'll excuse the expression.' She guffawed.

'Holly is taking the house.'

Caroline nodded. She straightened her sequined shirt and shook back her long hair. 'Of course. It's a nice house. But what about you? And Marilyn Beth? *And* Holly?'

'Why do you ask?'

'You know, Simon.' Caroline sipped her wine. Her party face had turned serious.

'What did Peter do after Babe died, Caroline? We'll survive.'

Caroline laughed harshly. 'Babe was no June. You know that. As much as he'd like to have been. As much as *I'd* like to have been. Who wouldn't like to be June McNellis? And God did I try. That was a long, long time ago. My God – it was a different universe.'

'We'll all survive, Caroline.'

'When Babe and I divorced, your mother and I had a long talk. She had always been on my side, you know. In the family. She even took my side against Babe.'

'I know.' Simon looked to the greenhouse. The others were engrossed in the news.

'But we argued. About kids. I said, "Peter is old enough, June," and she said . . . '

'I know. She told us a million times.'

'Let me continue.' Caroline moved from the counter toward Simon. Her taut, preserved face was suddenly angry. 'I said, "How long do children need their parents?" And you know what she said?'

'I know,' Simon said. 'She told us.'

'It was right here in this kitchen. She said, "My father is ninety-eight years old. I still need him. My son is twenty-two years old. He lives on the other side of the world, in Tokyo. *He* still needs me." That's what she said.'

'She's told us a million times.'

She flicked her long, black hair. 'It's a fantasy, Simon. It's a McNellis family fantasy. Don't tell me you believe it.'

Simon looked from the kitchen to the dining-room, to the gilded mirror, half-hoping for a thump, a quiver.

'How old are you now? Do you need your mother in New Delhi? Did you need her in Tokyo?'

Tokyo, thought Simon. *Not Tokyo.*

'Let's ask Peter,' Simon said harshly. 'C'mon. Let's call him now.'

Adrian, detecting conflict, loudly announced a new program. Fred, drink in hand, bellowed, 'I've *told* the networks. I was at Holy Cross with . . . ' Grace came to the kitchen. She stood next to Simon and exhaled as if exhausted. 'My train . . . '

'I think Bethy ought to drive you. On her way. If you don't mind.' They kissed good night. Grace walked heavily to the front door, clumsily winding a scarf around her neck. Fred was pushed to the front door, still talking, guided by Rhonda. She put her nose in Simon's ear and whispered, 'Don't worry! I'm driving!'

Holly returned from Vera Sherman's and in a rush announced, 'It's not anyone's grandmother's! Ruthie says they bought it in a second-hand shop. She couldn't give a shit about it.'

Simon explained to Caroline about the needlepoint.

'May.' Caroline shook her hair knowingly. She gave a dismissing laugh. She drained her wine and gave Holly a kiss on both cheeks. 'If she gets away with a needlepoint, the McNellises will be lucky. I lost Babe.' Caroline's fancy car was gone before Rhonda had managed to back out of the driveway, her stiff red hair swivelling nervously from side to side.

'I'm glad Caroline came,' Holly said.

'Yeah,' said Simon.

'I'm beat.' Adrian flicked off the television. He burped. 'There's nothing new on the Middle East, really. What *did* you put in those chickpeas?'

Dr Coughlin warned that when June's steroid renaissance ended, it would end abruptly and completely. Holly told the tale of a friend's mother, who had the same cancer.

'The same cancer?' asked Simon. 'It sounds like a car.'

'Her steroids pooped out after exactly two months. She was dead in days.'

Simon counted weeks on his fingers. 'What do we do?'

'We have to worry about the pain. Mom's complaining more. I think the pills aren't working. Did the hospice ever call back?'

'There was a call when I was sleeping. And wait: I thought the painkillers were too strong.'

Marilyn Beth rose from the table and stomped to the kitchen. 'Sometimes I wish she'd get run over by a truck.'

Across the table, Holly raised her eyebrows.

'A truck?' said Simon. 'It would have to come in through the front door to get near her, Bethy. It would have to find her bedroom.'

'I mean I just can't take it much longer. It's pathetic. The whole thing is pathetic. I'm never dying this way.'

Holly gave a sympathetic smile.

'Do tell, Bethy. How are you planning to die? In Mexico?'

'I'd rather go out with a bang.' Marilyn Beth pulled on

her white coat. She brought the two palms of her hand together in a clap, the long, lacquered nails extended stiffly. 'Whammo. Between the headlights of an eighteen-wheeler.'

June's coughing became terrible to hear. Simon was frequently awakened. He lay in bed listening. He rose, naked and cold, opened the den door as quietly as he could and called, 'Mom? Are you all right?' The coughing stopped. June responded affirmatively. The lights in her room blazed, as always, and her radio blared. Simon closed his door, locked it and slept again.

'I couldn't find those thin hamburger patties at Daitch,' Simon said. 'There aren't any more in the basement. I can't remember a time we didn't have them in the house.'

'You have to go to Pathmark,' Holly said. 'Speaking of, what's this scratchy toilet paper?'

'I didn't know Mom's brand. I'm not used to the selection. You should see the toilet paper in New Delhi.'

Holly told him the proper brand.

Simon was surprised. 'With the baby on the front? That's the most expensive.'

'You bought the cheapest.'

'I don't think it was the absolute cheapest. Is it that scratchy?'

On a blue-skied Sunday morning, Vera Sherman watched Simon McNellis emerge from the house, pulling his overcoat around his thin frame. He wore teenage-like jeans. He called through the open red door, steam pouring from his mouth. An unfamiliar woman emerged, tall, making an impatient gesture. She pointed to the sky and touched Simon's arm irritably. It took Vera several seconds to recognize Simon's friend Grace. She must have arrived the previous evening. They had all had dinner at June's house,

Vera knew. She had seen the arrival and departure of Holly and Marilyn Beth's cars. And, yes, there had been something dressy about Holly. Of course: she had worn low heels! Marilyn's thick hair had been pulled into a formal bun.

Grace withdrew into the house. In the distance, Simon's face was pale and rigid with the fresh cold. He looked remarkably like the young June McNellis. They had the same thin lips, the sculpted nose, the serious, recessed eyes, which, to Vera Sherman, seemed to penetrate the distance between the houses. She stepped back from her kitchen curtains. Grace reappeared wearing a long, brown coat. The two walked toward the old bridge at the creek. June didn't approve of Grace, Vera thought, or not 100%. She was too large, too self-aware, too judgmental. June had expected, and half-feared, Simon's return with an oriental bride. Vera knew. The hints had come over the telephone ever since Japan. But Simon had always returned alone. All that was behind the McNellises now. When the two returned, Grace and Simon had their arms loosely linked. To Vera's surprise, Simon was dragging on a cigarette. He threw it in the snow outside the house. They went inside the house, joking at the doorstep. They emerged before long, with Simon toting a white suitcase. Grace struggled with a black, man's umbrella. The car pulled off toward the station. When it returned, Vera was still watching. She saw Simon flick another cigarette into the snow. He exhaled steam mingled with smoke. He pushed through the red door with a practiced foot movement as old as his very life.

June was still getting to the dining-room table each evening. And she had hours of life. She took phone calls from Adrian. She got down a glass or two of wine, a Bloody Mary, a half-pancake. But mostly she sat staring at the small television on the dining-room cabinet. Each night she watched the same succession of evening sitcoms: one about a girl's dormitory, two about wisecracking American families.

At first Simon was critical of the shows. But one night, with an alien look, June had replied, 'They pass the time.' Her eyes sought the screen. Her hand groped for a cigarette. June had shrunk to bones and painted slashes beneath the gap-buttoned nightgown. Simon didn't comment again. Each night he watched the shows with her, a book before him. Occasionally he laughed and June felt forced to respond. She smiled dimly. It was an effort. So Simon stopped laughing.

Simon was unpacking sandwiches from Jerry's when he heard, from the greenhouse, Paul's unconscious singing. 'Mama's little baby loves shortnin' shortnin', Mama's little baby loves shortnin' bread.'

'I haven't heard that song in years.' Simon put his sandwich down. 'Do they still teach that to kids? How marvelous.'

'So many things are the same from our childhood,' Holly said. 'Especially the old cartoons. I watch them. The kids are amazed.'

'I loved the ones where the adults go to sleep at night and the things in the house come alive. In the kitchen.'

'Oh yes! They always had Fred Astaire and Ginger Rogers characters. Salt- and pepper-shakers.'

'And Jimmy Durante.'

'Jerry Colonna,' Holly laughed. 'I've never seen Jerry Colonna in a movie or a TV show. Just in the cartoons. Pop-eyed.'

'I had the most awful dream last night,' Simon said. 'My name was changed. I told someone, "I used to be called Simon." '

'What was your new name?'

'I can't remember. It was like the name of a car. Or a

country club. I told Mom I wanted back my old name. She said: "I *like* your new name, honey." '

'Creepy,' said Holly.

'I think this house is getting to me. The noises at night.' Holly talked about their plans to take over the house. She told Simon they could barely swing it financially. She suggested he become a partner. 'You can get the tax advantages,' she said. 'How else are you planning to invest your money?'

The next day Simon explained he'd get no tax advantage as an expatriate. 'As an investment, well, the market is going down.' Holly looked disappointed.

'I had another dream,' Simon said. 'I dreamt someone was trying to steal Grandma's ring from Mom's finger. In her bedroom.'

'A May dream,' said Holly. 'God help you. This house *must* be getting to you.'

Simon took a walk on another morning, when the weather was cold and drizzly. Vera Sherman watched from her kitchen window. He walked fast, with his hand holding his collar. He was away nearly an hour. When he returned, his hair was dark and wet.

Holly labored to get her boys into coats and shoes. Paul couldn't find his gloves. The red door was open on a steely evening. She closed it and said, 'Do you ever wonder whether their marriage was in trouble?'

'I have,' Simon said. 'I remember that big fight. When Doc and Grandma were here. I was sleeping in the den. It was summertime. I heard it.'

'And for years,' Holly said eagerly, 'Grandma and Grandpa stayed in that rental by the beach.'

Simon nodded thoughtfully. 'Is that why?'

'Was that the year Mom lost all that weight? Was it the same summer as the Dominican Republic?'

Simon concentrated. 'I can't remember. It seems earlier.'

'Because we all know now what that means. I mean why else do you lose so much weight?'

There was a banging noise. 'Oh God, I forgot her water.'

'I'll get it,' Simon said. 'You go. See you tomorrow.'

After dinner, Simon killed the jazz from the kitchen radio, armed the security system, shut the red door firmly and drove into town. He wondered whether Holly should be told the tale only he knew: the tale of Don's last night in the McNellis marriage bed. The bed that disappeared after his death, replaced by the single bed of June McNellis's widowhood. The tale that vanquished forever the 'perfection' of the McNellis family.

At Flip's, Marilyn Beth talked of her move to Cancun. 'The biggest thing is quitting. I can't wait to quit.'

'Wouldn't Mexico City be better? I mean for jobs?'

'Maybe,' she replied. 'But it doesn't have what Cancun has. To recreate.'

For a second, Simon thought she meant reproduce.

'Cancun has the beach. The only problem is with skiing. I'll have to fly to Colorado. Otherwise, I'll have everything I have right here.'

He asked her how long she was waiting after June died.

'Not long.' A group of her friends entered. Marilyn Beth cupped her hands to her mouth and yelled, 'Fuckin A!'

'It can be hard living abroad, you know.'

'It'll be worse here. I'm not going over to Mom's to find Holly and Kevin there. Oh my God. Hide me.' She shrunk down in her seat. 'My Spanish teacher.'

'Have you been missing classes?'

'Just the last few. Move your head over, would you? This way.'

Adrian started calling twice a day. So did Dr Coughlin. The hospice nurse arrived every evening at five and asked, in a gravely attentive tone, how things were. Simon canceled plans to go to a play with Grace. Adrian said he'd fly in on Wednesday. Holly said, 'Oh God: next week is the February vacation. Both boys will be out of school.' Every evening, Simon found a casserole dish on the front step, which he threw away without inspection. He stocked the house with easy food: expensive steaks, chops, frozen vegetables. He bought Ivory soap, toilet paper, discount shampoos. One day he bought paper plates, plastic cups and plastic cutlery for the party after the funeral. He put fresh sheets on the beds, soap throughout the house and a four-pack of toilet paper in each of the upstairs bathrooms.

Barbara called that evening with a plea. 'Keep me informed, kids, please. Just keep me informed. June's my oldest friend.'

On Tuesday, June didn't leave her bed. In the early evening, Simon insisted she try for the bathroom. She sat up with intense concentration. Her nightgown was hiked around her bone-colored hips. She gasped: 'Okay. Okay. Let's try.' He guided her slowly to the bathroom where she stayed for a lengthy time. Finally she called. When Simon eased her to her feet her face spasmed. 'Did you manage to go, Mom? Did you manage to go?' The short walk back to the bed was heart-poundingly slow. June's teeth chattered when he covered her with the blue comforter.

Simon called the hospice nurse. He returned to the bathroom. The toilet water was rust-colored. The nurse arrived. Simon described what happened and the nurse went to the bathroom. When she returned, she pulled a walkie-talkie from her handbag and murmured into it intently.

'Better get your sisters here.'

She called the pharmacy and ordered a long list of goods, including catheters and liquid morphine. 'I'm getting her a hospital bed,' she announced. 'At least let's get her comfortable.'

Simon went into June's room, amazed at its relative peacefulness. June leaned over and turned down the radio.

Her face was swollen, but the swelling had become familiar and sweet. She smiled.

'Recovered?'

She put a hand to her forehead. 'I guess so, honey. I didn't think I'd make it.'

'I think the nurse is changing the medication.'

June winced at a new pain. Holly entered the room in her coat. She smiled at her mother. 'How are you feeling?'

'Not so bad now.'

'Want some water?'

'Yes.'

Holly tugged at Simon's sleeve. They went to the bathroom. While the water ran into the tumbler, Holly whispered, 'The nurse.' She pointed to the living-room and made an injecting motion into her bicep. 'She's teaching us. Now.'

Marilyn Beth was sitting at her place, fiddling with a thick brown bottle. She held it up. 'The real thing! Enough to get us all high.'

'Enough to get us all dead,' said the nurse. 'Allow me please.'

The nurse demonstrated how to fill the syringe and how to squirt a drop from the needletip. 'That's just for you. There's no way air bubbles are getting into your mother.' Then she showed how to inject. She pinched the freckled skin on Marilyn Beth's bicep. 'Just under the skin. That's all you have to worry about. Then you rub. Just like this.'

Simon decided to take the night duties. The injections were necessary every four hours; the first didn't begin until the pills wore off at midnight.

'I'll move in tomorrow night,' Holly said. 'We can share.'

'I'd love to give the first dose,' said Marilyn Beth. 'The last time I did this was when we castrated mice in psychology. You didn't have to stitch them up. You just pressed their little scrotums together. Like this. Amazing.'

'Amazing,' said Holly.

'Amazing,' said Simon.

'Shut up.' Marilyn Beth extended her chin and pulled the rubber band from her ponytail. 'Both of you.' She shook her thick hair over her shoulders. '*I'm* ready for a beer.'

'Me too,' said Holly.

'Me too,' said Simon.

Holly let in the delivery boys from the pharmacy. They carried four large black garbage-bags of health-care products. 'What's this?' asked Marilyn. 'God – it's a bedpan. Look at this color!'

One of the boys said, 'Where do you want the bed?'

'Follow me,' Holly said.

June was sleeping, so the children decided to give her a final night in her own bed. The pharmacy boys lifted her bed and placed it in the corner. They averted their glances from the unmoving sick woman. The hospital bed was given the pride of place beneath June's favorite floral painting. As they assembled it, with its wires and pistons, the boys chatted in a practiced, low voice. Their eyes never strayed to the woman in the corner, waxen-faced and yellow-haired. They ignored the room's foul smell. Finally they were done. Holly said, 'Thanks a lot. Really.' June raised her swollen eyelids. 'Thank you,' she said. Her arm lifted. The two boys bowed awkwardly.

'We'll move you tomorrow, Mom,' said Holly.

June said, 'I don't care.' The room was an odd spectacle: the big, empty, important hospital bed. In the corner, out of lamplight, the diminished bed of June McNellis's widowhood, hardly visible, containing the jewel that everyone was searching for, growing too lusterless for anyone to find or even want.

'We'd better call Adrian,' Holly said.

'Where's his hotel number?'

'On the pad in the kitchen. And what about May?'

'May's not coming until it's all over.' Simon juggled address books. 'I don't care what Adrian says.'

The doorbell rang.

'It must be the pharmacy again,' said Marilyn Beth. 'I'll get it.'

'Oh my God,' said Holly. 'It's Mrs Hanson. We told her she could come tonight.'

'Mrs Hanson?' Simon put down the phone. 'It's impossible. Mom's dying!'

'We put her off for so long.'

'Too long,' said Marilyn Beth. 'Tell her to come back next week. Ha, ha.'

Mrs Hanson was unchanged from the McNellises' childhood. She was tall, gourd-shaped, with limp hair so thin you could see pink scalp. Her scared look hadn't changed. Hansons had been in each of the McNellises' classes; each of the children gave an identical smile when she shuffled in the door. She said, 'Mom's feeling better?' She handed Marilyn Beth a casserole dish.

'I'll take that,' said Simon. The casserole had a piece of electrical tape on its side with letters reading: HANSON. Holly took her colorless raincoat.

'Debbie's a newscaster now. On Philly Four. She's seen your name, Don.' Mrs Hanson had always called Simon by his father's name.

'Give her my best,' said Simon.

'Come on Mrs Hanson,' said Holly. 'Let's see Mom.'

June was huddled near the wall. Holly pulled a chair toward June's bed. With her thigh she shoved the shiny, foam-covered hospital bed. 'We're moving her tomorrow. Mom. Mom? Mrs Hanson's here.'

Holly and Marilyn Beth helped June shift. She lay on her side. Holly smoothed her hair. Marilyn Beth turned off the radio.

Mrs Hanson faltered. 'Hello, uh, June.' She descended abruptly to the chair.

June's voice was weak. 'Hello Mary. Thank you for . . . ' She started to cough.

'I ran into Ed Coughlin at Christmas, June. He said you were holding up just fine.'

June continued to cough. Marilyn Beth said, 'Let's get some water.'

June's hand raised. 'Okay,' she said. 'It's okay. How are the children, Mary?'

'They're all fine, June.'

'How's . . . ' June looked to Simon. Her eyelids were thick and swollen.

'Debbie's in news in Philadelphia. Isn't that right, Mrs Hanson?'

'That's right. Doin' great.'

'Good,' said June. Her eyes closed slowly.

'I had to come by,' said Mary Hanson.

June's thick eyes opened again. 'Thank you Mary. Say hello . . . '

'Sleep, Mom,' said Simon.

'Okay. Okay.'

On the way out, Simon restored the askew hospital bed. At the front door, his sisters saw Mrs Hanson off. Marilyn Beth offered her a drink. Holly said, 'Coffee? Tea?' She refused and wrung her umbrella with nervous hands. 'It's just a tuna casserole,' she said. 'The kids used to love it. On Fridays. In the old days. You remember those, don't you Don? Who can believe it now?'

Simon asked about the democrats. 'They come through,' she said. 'That's something to say for them. They do come through. I was so glad when they dedicated that tree to your dad.'

'A tree?'

'At the golf course,' said Holly. 'You've seen it, Simon.'

'I never go by it,' said Mrs Hanson, 'without thinking of him. He always reminded me of Gary Cooper.'

When the door shut, Marilyn Beth said, 'Oh God.' They returned to the dining-room table. Simon got three fresh beers. Holly checked June. When she returned, she said, 'Well?'

'Good old Mom.' Simon shook his head. 'Good to the end. I was proud of her.'

Marilyn gulped the beer. 'Gary Cooper? I wonder if Mrs Hanson was hitting on Daddy all those years.'

'Daddy deserved Mrs Hanson,' Holly said, and the three McNellises laughed.

Simon stayed awake until midnight listening to the cool jazz from the kitchen. At the dining-room table he prepared June's first shot of morphine. His hands trembled, one holding the squat bottle of fluid, the other balancing the feathery syringe with its tumescent needle. A drop glistened from the top and he carried the syringe, upturned and at eye level, into the bedroom.

'Mom?'

June stirred slowly. He swabbed her dry bicep. The needle went in effortlessly. He pushed the plunger, expecting a reaction but there was none. He extracted the needle and put the syringe on the edge of the bed. He tried to swab June's arm with alcohol. But he couldn't find the needle mark in the tissue-paper wrinkles.

June's eyes remained closed. She spoke in a low voice. 'It must feel funny to do that.'

'It does.'

June nodded slightly. 'I bet.' She gave a short cough.

'That should feel better. It's not much stronger than the pills, just injected. I'll give you another in a few hours.'

She nodded.

'Do you want some water?'

June shook her head. She sighed, as if the drug was already taking effect.

Simon turned off the lights, set the security system and went to the den. The house made its strained protests against the cold. He set his alarm and fell asleep. In June McNellis's bedroom, the lights continued to blaze. The children had forgotten to pull the blinds: the rectangles of light on the far beeches were brighter than ever before. The dying woman was pushed in a corner, removed from her sleeping place of thirty-five years. If she had opened her eyes she would have seen an unfamiliar patch of wall-paper containing oddly passionate flowers. Green vines twisted to the ceiling, intertwined with red, cone-like flowers. The vines throbbed with a new sap: clear, power-ful, timeless. Fresh leaves of pale, fragile green sprouted. The view from that dark corner lifted slowly to the ceiling, shadow turned to light, and the room had a different aspect. The large blue hospital bed dominated. Pushed to the wall was a monk's cot with a delicate wooden head-board and a negligible lump lying beneath a worn comfor-ter. The vines bloomed with the new sap: there was laugh-ter in many voices, all sounding the same. A wedding day, a tight white bonnet of feathers that cost a small fortune. There was an apartment with bars on the windows. A red convertible. Horses, a man in the bushes, pants open to display a thick purple penis and folds of gray underwear. More laughter, girlish screams, horses flying away. A man walked through the shallow aqua waters carrying a child on his shoulders. It was Don; above him Marilyn Beth. In the river, on a rock, his legs scissored and flashing that incredible smile. Coconuts with straws out the top, her first rum sour. 'In this climate, rum is the only thing you can survive.' Somebody pulled at her engagement ring; the lump under the comforter resisted. Don's hateful pull on a summer night and June's stifled cry: 'They'll hear us. Upstairs!' Their walk to the old bridge, green vines

124

protruding through its iron bars, how he pulled her again. And that hateful Tokyo lane where the boy-man strode angrily away, down jacket swinging. He looked back with tears in his eyes. Her eyes. She stood in her fur coat, the cold pouring in, a vanquished sun in the process of cooling. June's universe would never be the same. The orbits would never again be so tight, so perfectly circular. Don's hip: she felt it in the small of her back, could see it in her mind, its fine-etched hairs, could feel it move away, disappear, see the bathroom light flash on the far wall, the flowers, and then die. The bedroom door shut gently and the car started up and Don went away. She lay in their bed unmoving. But the children were *hers*. That would never change. They stood before her shrinking to teenagers, to toddlers, to babies. She realized it was all going backwards. The vines were shrivelling, fading and she shut her eyes before the flowers dropped and the lovely new leaves withered. The sap was falling. The view from the ceiling receded until there was nothing left but a patch of wallpaper and a small cobweb Holly had missed in her attempt to keep the McNellis house in perfect order. June struggled to move, to rise from the narrow bed, to flare once more, but she could barely stir. She spoke and the words came out wrong and weak, a stupid, sleepy whisper. 'Okay guys . . . ' Then the morphine took final hold and June McNellis slept.

At four a.m., Simon awoke. He looked in on his mother and went to the dining-room to prepare the second injection. He did it with confident hands, enjoying it. He gave June the injection. In the bathroom he filled a glass of water and took from a clear bag a blue drinking-straw. 'Mom? Some water?' June managed a sip through flaking lips. He swabbed her gums with a tiny sponge on a stick, as the nurse had recommended.

'You feel alright? No pain?'

June gave a barely perceptible nod.

Simon went back to the den, locked the door and set the alarm for seven-thirty.

June's bedroom, when Simon entered it, was so starkly changed that he halted in alarm. He blurted, 'Mom?'

The hospital bed was the main change. But there was an acrid, repulsive smell filling the room. He went to the window and opened it wide. Cold poured in. He looked to the tiny figure under the comforter and lowered the window halfway. The wallpaper seemed oddly prominent: fleshy red flowers on vines. Simon realized the blinds had been left up the evening before and the windows filled the room with soft, winter light. And the bedroom was silent. The radio had been switched off. No one had thought to put it back on.

He prepared the third injection in the dining-room and administered it. June breathed with a strange noise. He went to the kitchen and dialled Holly's number.

'Oh God,' she said. 'It sounds like Daddy.'

'I'll call Bethy.'

'Call Adrian.'

Holly arrived in record time. She went straight to June's room without removing her coat.

'Maybe I shouldn't have given her that shot.'

'I don't think it matters. Did you call Coughlin? She sounds just like Daddy.'

Marilyn Beth arrived and they conferred at the dining-room table.

'I think we have to call May,' said Holly. 'It's time.'

'You do it,' said Simon.

'I'll do it,' said Marilyn Beth. 'I'd love to do it.'

'Let's call Coughlin first.' But Coughlin said nothing could be done. He promised to come over after lunch.

'After lunch?' scoffed Marilyn Beth. 'Thanks a lot.'

They went to June's room. Simon said, 'Let's get this fucking bed out of the way.' They pushed the blue hospital bed under the windows and, lifting gingerly, restored June's bed to its rightful place beneath the floral painting.

'Oh, Mom,' said Holly.

June was breathing hard.

'What's that smell?' whispered Marilyn Beth. 'Is it the cancer? From the lungs? Or the stomach?'

The phone rang. 'Don't get it here,' whispered Holly. 'Get it in the kitchen.'

The call was from Vera Sherman. When Simon hung up, it rang again. Adrian announced he was catching the first plane. He asked about May. Simon called the hospice and Barbara. Finally he dialled May's number.

'Oh, *darlin*! Carmen and I have been just sitting here worryin! We had two guests last night who demanded a discount. How's Mum?'

They restored June's bedroom to normal. Simon removed the radio and the mystery novels June had ceased reading weeks earlier. The blue hospital bed, against the wall, provided a handy seating place. Holly opened all the blinds and a second window. 'I have an air freshener at home. Kevin can bring it.'

'God no,' said Simon. 'No Glade.'

'It's imported.'

June made a choking sound. 'I don't think she's going to make it to lunch,' Simon said. 'Look.'

'What about the pain?'

'I gave the injection at eight. Seven forty-five. Seven-forty.'

In the dining-room, Marilyn Beth wondered whether to go to work for the morning.

'I don't think she's going to make it through lunch,' Simon said. 'I really don't.'

The morning progressed with extraordinary slowness. June lay on her back, waxen-faced, her mouth in a twisted oval. Holly smoothed June's hair and said, 'Oh Mom.' Holly and Simon took turns checking the bedroom. Marilyn Beth sat in the dining-room, as when Don died, taking the phone calls. Every few minutes, Simon said, 'Her breathing's changed.' All three rushed into the room. But they were false alarms.

'I hate this,' said Marilyn Beth. 'I should have gone to work.'

Simon and Holly sat with their mother. Simon opened one of the drawers of the white wicker dresser.

'God, there's a lot of junky jewelry.'

'The good stuff's in the kitchen. In a brown paper bag. Except for grandma's ring.' Holly petted June's hand. 'I wish she could give some sign. A squeeze.'

'She has an extra wallet.' Simon rooted through the drawer. 'Two. She must have bought them in bulk.'

'At Odd Lots.'

'You're right. There's a tag. $6.99.'

Simon opened another drawer. 'Here's that stupid wig.' He put it on. 'Remember when we used to put this on Bethy?'

'The pictures are in the picture box. Whatever happened to that grass skirt?' June choked alarmingly. She sunk back into her normal gasps. Simon threw the wig into the drawer. 'What about these rosary beads? Should we put one in her hand?'

'Oh Simon, I hate that kind of thing. Christ! We forgot to call a priest.'

Marilyn Beth was deputed to call the church. The lines were busy. She drove to fetch one.

Simon went back to the drawers. 'Here are Daddy's electronic things. God he had a lot of them.'

'All those trips to Hong Kong.'

'Ah ha!' Simon held aloft a chrome cuticle clipper. 'I can't tell you how many times I've needed one of these. Do they still make them?' He rummaged further. 'She has two.'

They heard the sound of the front door and a loud, familiar voice.

'It's Barbara.' Holly whispered as if hiding the news from June. 'Go!'

Simon found Barbara standing at the front door. She was dressed in slacks and a black turtleneck sweater. She enfolded him in strong arms. She took his face in her hands. 'I came as fast as I could. I almost cracked up. I was crying, like this.' She moved her fingers down her cheeks. 'The man in the next car thought I was nuts. Where's my June?'

'Come on Barbara. Come see Mom.'

At the bedroom door, Barbara grabbed Simon's arm. 'Oh my God.' Holly smiled from the bedside, holding June's hand. She motioned.

Simon pulled Barbara's hand. 'Come.'

Barbara moved slowly to the bed. 'Oh June.' She bent and kissed her cheek. She smoothed June's thin hair. The breathing became harder. 'June, what has happened to you? June McNellis. Sweet Jesus in heaven. What you *do* to us!'

The front door sounded again. Vera Sherman arrived at the bedroom door. 'I saw Barbara's car.'

'I can't believe this.' Barbara spoke in a loud whisper. 'Can you believe this Vera? Oh kids: I'm so grateful you called. I'm so glad you let me come.'

'Get comfortable,' said Holly. 'She's been like this all morning.'

Vera looked at the children. 'How's everyone doing? How's Marilyn Beth?'

'She's gone to the church.'

'I saw her car.'

'This is just unbelievable,' said Barbara. 'I watched my parents die and my aunts but this is something else. Oh June: poor baby!'

Simon opened the window further. 'There's a bad smell.'

Marilyn Beth arrived, followed by a priest with a mustache. He kissed his halter and performed a hurried Extreme Unction. June choked throughout it. Everyone thanked him and Marilyn Beth showed him to the door. She went out for sandwiches. Vera and Barbara refused food. Simon said, 'I'm hungry as a horse.' Barbara said, 'Well, if no one's eating this sausage-and-pepper.' Kevin arrived with a tiny spray can with floral-patterned label. He and Holly spent time with June. He left the house reluctantly with large, dangling hands.

Vera returned to her house. Barbara alternated between the bedroom and the dining-room. Holly and Simon took turns in June's room. Holly's spray half-defeated the odor. There were several false alarms but finally Simon called from the bedroom, 'Gang. Come here. I think this is it.'

Marilyn Beth stood on one side of the bed. Holly and Barbara took the other. Simon stood at its foot. 'It's different, isn't it?'

'It's different,' said Holly.

Barbara smoothed June's hair. 'Oh Junie.'

June stopped breathing. They stared at her waxen face, afraid to look at each other. Then she took an ugly, cobwebbed breath.

'Mom,' said Marilyn Beth. 'If you do that again . . .'

Barbara bent at the waist with restrained laughter. 'It's awful, but my God, June!' Barbara spoke in her loud whisper. 'She was always like that. You should have seen her at college!'

Holly sprayed again. Soon all rhythm broke down. June's eyelids fluttered. The children craned their heads, hoping she could see.

Vera Sherman moved quietly into the room. She circled around Simon and stood next to Marilyn Beth. She squeezed her arm. June McNellis took a last, labored breath. They waited. Several seconds later, the yellowed, waxen face paled horribly. Simon said, 'God. How could we have been fooled before?'

Marilyn Beth leaned forward and, for the first time, smoothed her mother's hair. 'Go to Daddy, Mom.' She bent down and kissed her dead lips.

They stood awkwardly, touching June's hair and her hands. Simon said, 'That's it for me.' He moved to the head of the bed, pecked at his mother's forehead and went to the windows. He opened them wide. He returned to the dining-room and opened June's address book. He picked up the telephone. Marilyn Beth and Holly followed. It was not yet dusk but Holly said, 'I want a beer.' Barbara and Vera Sherman remained in the bedroom until the hospice workers arrived with their gear. Then everyone gathered in the kitchen, afraid of what they might witness going out the front door.

'I'm so glad you kids allowed me here.' Barbara enfolded Marilyn Beth in her arms. 'Godchild.'

'Godmother!' Marilyn Beth wiped tears with her free hand.

'What did you do in there?' asked Simon.

'We were saying goodbye,' said Barbara. 'We cried. We laughed.'

Vera, hands folded before her, nodded serenely. 'I had the spray can.'

The rest of the night was dedicated to informing June

McNellis's friends and family. The three children, keyed up, competed to make the calls. Simon said, 'That was Harriet. They're *not* coming for the funeral. I expected a bit more from her.'

'I couldn't get Winston Rubenoff off the phone,' said Holly. 'He started blubbering.'

'Winston *Rubenoff*?' said Marilyn Beth. 'I hope *he's* not coming.'

Simon plugged in the hospital bed and Jeremy and Paul played with it, riding it up and down. He and Marilyn Beth cleaned June's room, covering the bed with the white spread that had gone unused since June's illness. Holly chose one of her mother's dresses from the closet. She put a tube of lipstick in a paper bag and pinned it onto the dress. She marked the bag: June McNellis. 'Her Nancy Reagan dress,' said Simon. Marilyn Beth drove it to the funeral home.

Adrian arrived with his Irish hat and a disappointed look. But he quickly got involved in the writing of June's obituary. The local paper phoned back with questions. Adrian explained he was a former journalist. He got off the phone chuckling.

'He asked for a quote about June. A "sparkler."' Adrian bit into a slice of pizza. ' "She was taller than the highest redwood! Deeper than the deepest sea!" '

'Those journalists,' said Simon.

'He was happy with the fashion-model angle.'

'You didn't bring that up?' said Holly. 'Mom would shit.'

They discussed May's arrival later that night. Marilyn Beth agreed to pick her up at the airport.

'You're in my room, Adrian,' said Simon. 'May can have the girls' room. I'd like to stay in the den.'

'Why?' asked Holly.

'I feel better near Mom's room.'

The girls departed and Adrian decided to watch the

late news. 'Here, Simon, there's something on the Middle East.'

Simon went through the house gathering plastic vials from June's bedroom, her bathroom and the kitchen. He threw them all in the kitchen garbage can.

'Those syringes can be used,' said Adrian. 'What are these? Laxatives?'

'Fuck them,' said Simon. 'They're all going – once and for all.'

May arrived many hours later to a dead house. June's bedroom was dark: the light from the hallway showed a tiny bed, a pure, smooth, white bedspread. Later, in the blackened girls' room and in the midst of a dream, May was awakened by a noise. She sat up and grasped her blanket. Her hands fingered her face. Someone had entered her bedroom.

'Adrian? Simon darlin?' She peered toward the door and then to the small entrance to the attic closet.

Another noise came. It was a house noise. A winter wind rushed outside the windows. May fell back onto her pillow. But she couldn't sleep. Her dream troubled her. It had taken place in June's bedroom: the lights burning, the radio blaring, the shades pulled, the dying woman curled oblivious on the bed. It was the bedroom May had known at Christmas. June slept peacefully. May examined the photos on her dresser and noticed, as she had several times before, the silver, scallop-shaped dish with the flowery 'M' in the middle. 'I just love this photo of Dad.' But June snored peacefully. May raised the dish. It resisted with admirable heaviness. She tucked it beneath her small, black jacket. She inclined her head a fraction to find June staring at her from the bed, a cigarette in hand, ash dangling over the carpet.

'It's plate,' June said. 'Don't waste your time.'

135

'Ghastly.' May's whisper died in the darkness. The wind roared. Plate – preposterous. The dish was too heavy. She turned in bed and it struck her: had June been carried off with the damn diamond on her skinny finger? Were the children such nincompoops? Because everyone knew what they'd do with it. Even if it was returned, days later, the stone would be switched and artificial diamonds were too good these days. May, had she been called in time, would have tearfully removed the ring when it was all over, or, possibly, during a peaceful moment before the damn priest arrived. Possibly, quietly, the evening before. During a lull. Yes, the evening before would have been perfect. June would hardly have noticed or minded – she might have preferred it that way. May brought her hands to her face, which helped her sleep. But sleep eluded May for a long time and the house noises roared on, underscored by a growing wind outside. May pulled the blankets closer and hoped for warmth.

On the morning after his mother's death, Simon McNellis awoke to strong light pounding through the paper blinds of the den. He raised a blind and found woods, clean and green, crowned by a lucid blue sky. He unlocked his door and walked across the hall to June's room. It was unaltered. He smoothed the white bedspread. Watery sounds came from June's bathroom. Its door was closed.

'May?'

There was a pause. The water ceased. 'Yes darlin?'

Simon put his hand on the wall. 'You got in.'

There was another pause. 'I don't know what went wrong, darlin, it was . . . ' He heard a scrabbling at the doorknob. 'Marilyn Beth wasn't at the airport.' The door opened a crack. May's little face, a towel around her head, appeared. She smiled with small, pale eyes. 'Kevin darlin had to come fetch me.'

'You called Kevin? In the middle of the night?'

May nodded, wide-eyed.

Simon turned away. 'This kind of thing happens.' He went to the dining-room and picked up the phone. Marilyn Beth answered after nine rings.

'What happened for God's sake?'

'*I* was there. I didn't see May anywhere. Holly called at the most ungodly hour.'

Simon heard the furnace strain in the basement. He thought of the long day ahead, the wake, the funeral the next day. He saw the browned, leveled garden beyond the back window. June McNellis was no more.

'These things happen,' he said. 'You're coming over?'

Adrian came down in his jogging clothes. 'Can I tempt you, Sime?' May arrived in the kitchen, dressed and thickly made up. 'I can't imagine what happened,' she said. She rustled through the refrigerator and the pantry.

'There's nothing there,' Simon called from the dining-room table. 'We'll shop this morning.'

Holly and the boys arrived and everyone moved restlessly around the house. Simon and Holly rendezvoused in June's room.

'Did Bethy fuck up?'

Holly whispered. 'They changed the terminal a few months back. That's what Kevin says. Maybe Marilyn went to the wrong place. Or maybe she didn't go at all.'

'I'm sure May screwed it up somehow.'

'Let's get her out of here. We can send her shopping.'

'She was showering!' Simon pointed at June's bathroom. 'In Mom's bathroom.'

Holly grimaced. 'I wonder if we'll ever get rid of that smell.'

'You'll have to strip the plaster.'

Holly looked at her watch. 'Tell the pharmacy to take back all their stuff.' She grasped the handles of the wheelchair and shoved it at Simon. 'This has leg attachments in the basement.'

May was sent to shop for provisions and fresh ferns for the greenhouse. June's had withered overnight. May was excited by her mission. 'Odd Lots had *wonderful* paper things in December.' She twisted the hair at her ears. 'Do you think this is enough, darlin?'

Marilyn Beth came for lunch. 'Don't blame me,' she

138

said. '*I* was there. And I don't care if May had to walk. What's the drill tonight?'

'We get there at seven-thirty. They'll leave the casket open for us. When we're finished, they'll close it. The rest come at eight.'

'They didn't do that with Daddy,' said Simon.

'Mom nixed it. You know how she felt.'

'Daddy would *not* have looked good in a coffin,' said Marilyn Beth. 'God – there's *nothing* in this house to eat.'

Holly vacuumed with vigor. Simon collected stray things, which he jammed in closets and drawers. In the kitchen, Holly dumped an armful of small silver articles onto the counter. A napkin ring rolled into the sink.

'Mom warned us.' Holly pulled a brown grocery bag from beneath the sink and swept the silver into it.

'That?'

'Our heirlooms.' Holly folded the bag several times and replaced it. 'Haven't you seen Marilyn Beth going through it? She does it just about every other Saturday.'

In the den, Simon called Holly. She appeared with filled arms.

'What's this crap?' He gestured to a pile of cloth cuttings and foam pieces on the floor.

'They're my cushions. For the living-room. Just put them in the closet.'

One of the articles in Holly's arms was *Decorating Rich*. Simon grabbed it and hurled it into the closet. After it he piled the foam and fabric.

'We'll have to clean this out later.'

'We can burn the damn book.' Simon slammed the closet door. 'Dancing around the flame. What will we do with May's clothes? She'll never be able to lug them all back.'

'It's not our problem anymore,' Holly said. 'Mom's dead. That whole chapter is ended.'

May returned from her foraging. Simon carried the ferns from the car.

'I was going to call from the nursery, darlin. I thought thirty dollars was too much, but look how beautiful they are! Mum would have loved them. She'd have paid forty!' She unloaded bags from a range of different stores. The kitchen counter filled with muffins, purple and pink wrapping-paper, squat jars of preserves.

'Look at this darlin. Have you ever tried it?' She held a small, white sack of coffee. 'This is vanilla-flavoured and that one is cinnamon. Doesn't that sound wonderful? I can't wait until tomorrow morning! We'll all have to get up early! Before Mum's funeral!'

Adrian fiddled with the kitchen radio. 'Maybe we can get June's favorite call-in show. I hear they're having a special memorial program. June was their most loyal listener.' He lowered his voice, as if June might be listening. 'I couldn't believe the way she listened to that radio. Sometimes it was hard to sleep!'

'They'll discuss her sex life,' said Simon. 'I don't think we want to listen to that.'

'Oh, it was wonderful, darlin.' May's hands danced across the table toward Simon. 'Mum *told* me. She said your father was just . . . ' Marilyn Beth interrupted with a deliberate comment about the funeral home and the director's son, who had been in her class. Simon walked from the table. He retreated to June's bedroom. When he returned, May had disappeared. In the kitchen, Holly held a packet of coffee. 'This cost four dollars twenty nine.' Adrian was staring at a jar of lemon preserves. 'This is pretty pricey too. May has expensive taste. Babe always said so.'

'On Mom's money,' Simon said.

'Our money,' said Holly.

In the afternoon, Simon retired to his room. He locked the door, pulled the paper blinds and lay down on the bed. He adjusted his underpants and tried to masturbate but none of his images succeeded. Even the Japanese woman, that painful, potent memory, refused to fill his mental screen. He stroked vigorously but came feebly – a few clear drops, not enough to wipe away. But he slept deeply.

At dusk, Simon was the only one awake. The house was still but not lonely. Watery light filled the living- and dining-rooms. Life still coursed throughthe McNellis house. Simon pulled the front curtains and the back drapes in homage to his mother. He retuned the kitchen radio; jazz oozed comfortingly. He collected the last of the scattered toys from the greenhouse and threw them in a drawer. He went to June's bedroom, once again satisfied by its healthy tidiness. The bathroom was in order, with new towels, and he shut its door. On the dresser he found photos in familiar frames. His father in the swirling waters; his mother's wedding picture, lovely in a cap of white feathers; the McNellis children, dark-eyed and light-haired. He picked up the scalloped dish and opened June's dresser drawer. He shut it and brought the dish to his room, where he locked it in his suitcase.

Adrian was at the dining-room table with a glass of milk. He bragged about an unusually successful nap. Holly came through the front door in a black dress. She dumped the local paper on the table. 'Page twenty-two.' Adrian read aloud June's obituary, satisfied except for the single misprint.

'Christian Count College. It sounds like Dracula's school.'

In the greenhouse, Simon said, 'Holly?'

Holly looked from the kitchen. Simon held May's roll of purple wrapping-paper like a javelin. He chucked it down the cellar staircase. He did the same with the pink roll.

'Is Winston Rubenoff really coming?' Adrian flipped the

pages of the paper. 'What must he look like after all these years?'

Simon said he expected a rough wake. Holly produced a vial of pills. Simon looked at them and passed them to Adrian.

'Are you guys turning into junkies?'

'Mom got them for Daddy's funeral.'

Simon checked the date: it was 1986. 'Did Mom use them?'

'I don't remember June taking any pills,' said Adrian. 'Ever.'

'There's only one way to tell.' Simon opened the vial and counted the pills. There were thirty, as cited on the label.

'I knew I hadn't seen June taking any pills,' said Adrian.

'She took one when she yelled at Mrs Witt,' said Holly. 'Let's not forget that historic occasion.'

'Have you taken any yet?'

'Nope,' said Holly. 'But I might.'

'Keep them close,' Simon said.

Marilyn Beth arrived, her hair pulled into a bun. May descended, heavily made up. Adrian re-read June's obituary. 'Too bad they don't run photos.' Everyone laughed. 'An old picture. That's what I meant. One of her modeling pictures.'

'In a bathing-suit,' said Marilyn Beth.

'Where *are* Mum's weddin pictures?' May asked. 'I've been just dyin to get my hands on them.'

Holly and Simon drove to the funeral home together. They were met at the door by a poker-faced young man with wetted blonde curls. A gold pin secured his collar. He said, with a comical frown, 'These are the votive cards. A hundred and fifty.'

They nodded and walked past him.

'Isn't he awful?'

Holly whispered, 'Joe Studman, according to Marilyn.'

142

'She had a lot of studmen in that class,' said Simon. 'Look at him now: Morgue Studman.'

'Mr McNellis.' Simon turned back to the young man. 'It's Parlor A.'

'Thank you.' He whispered to Holly, 'Can't get enough of that young, vibrant flesh, throbbing with life . . . '

'Stop it.'

The home was subdued country-house, gold and green wallpaper with duck prints in undersized frames. There was a small notice board with movable plastic letters reading 'McNellis.' It stood next to a door with paned glass and curtains on the inside.

'Let's do it,' said Simon. He opened the door.

'Look at the flowers,' Holly said.

June was in a raised coffin at the far end of the room. The sight robbed Simon of all thought. He stopped halfway through the room and turned back to Holly: a boy in a dark suit with a face drained of color.

'Are you okay?'

'Of course,' he said. 'Come on.'

They proceeded to the coffin. Holly looked down: 'Oh Mom, what's wrong with your cheeks?'

'This isn't right.'

June was in her red and black suit. Enormous arrangements of flowers surrounded her.

'I've never seen anything like this,' said Simon. 'Can we pull this lid down?'

'Simon, *they* have to do it.'

'I'm sorry.' He walked stiffly to the door. In the hallway, Marilyn Beth and Adrian were being greeted by the funeral-home host.

'I'll be right back.' Simon wandered through the home, through a room with *People* magazines on a coffee table and found a men's room. He unfastened his pants and sat on the toilet. He wiped his forehead with tissue paper. When he returned, Holly said, 'Where are you going?'

143

'Some air.' Kevin was just arriving, stamping his shoes.

From the sidewalk, Simon watched the cars go by, glossily beautiful in the dry winter cold. He opened his suit jacket to expose his damp shirt. When the nausea receded he went back to the hallway. He kissed Vera Sherman.

'I drove May down. She's gone in.' Vera stood outside the room shyly. Finally Marilyn Beth, Adrian, May, Holly and Kevin abandoned Parlor A. The man with the wetted curls nodded significantly and removed himself through the doors, shutting them firmly behind him.

'Nail it down,' Simon said loudly.

'I don't think we should pay.' Marilyn Beth plumped her thick bun. 'Her face looks like Silly Putty.'

'She's looked better,' Adrian whispered. 'They never seem to do it *right*.'

'I've never seen anything more disgusting in my life,' Simon said.

Vera smiled sympathetically. 'Ross looked like his brother Mike. And that's no compliment. Everyone said so.'

'Except Mike,' said Adrian. 'Mike thought he looked great. Better than ever. We're just joking Vera.'

The man with the wetted curls emerged with a grim expression, as if June had given him a struggle. He opened the paned doors. The coffin at the far end was closed. Flowers were placed on top. Holly and Marilyn Beth circled the room reading the cards.

'Here's Winston Rubenoff's,' said Marilyn Beth. 'I hope that means he isn't coming.'

'Our blanket of roses is perfect.' The ivory buds hung over the lid of June's casket. Holly put her hand to her face. 'Mom would have just loved it.' Simon put his arm around Holly's shoulder.

'June McNellis!' A mannish yell came from the rear of the room. 'Don't tell me you're in that *box* June McNellis.' Barbara, coatless, stood in the doorway. Her hands sliced the air above her head. Her face was a Mediterranean mask with black, drooping eyes.

The three McNellises gathered around her, all talking at once. May was peering at flower cards through bifocals. She looked up with wide, black eyes. Barbara bent athletically at the waist. Her laugh split the room. 'Silly Putty?' she roared. 'I haven't heard of Silly Putty in years!'

With suddenness, the airless, flower-stuffed room filled. A man in a clerical collar pulled at Simon's sleeve. 'I'm here for prayers. *If* the family desires.' He had greasy strings of hair pulled across a bald head.

Simon looked at him with surprise. 'Wait a minute.' He interrupted Holly's conversation with Barbara. 'Do we want prayers? There's a priest up there. By Mom.'

'Absolutely not.' Holly turned back to Barbara.

'I'm sorry father. We don't need any.'

'Actually, I'm Brother William. I'm a Christian Brother.'

'An Irish Christian Brother?'

Brother William nodded piously.

'I was taught by Irish Christian Brothers.'

Brother William was pleased. 'You must have vivid memories of the Christian Brothers.'

'Indeed,' said Simon. 'None of them nice. Good night Brother William.' He turned to find Gerta with tears streaming down her face. She gave him a short, powerful hug. 'Ilya – he was in this same room!' She blew her nose and went to the casket to pray. Simon spotted Mario, Don's tennis friend, pulling at Adrian's arm. He was weeping. His wife was at the door talking animatedly to Vera Sherman. Simon went to Holly. 'I got rid of the priest.'

'Good,' said Holly. 'My God – who's that in the wheelchair?'

'It's Mom's wheelchair,' Simon said. 'They've rented it out already.'

Marilyn Beth rushed over. 'That's Angelica Witt. And her mother.'

'Lydia Witt?' Holly spoke with awe. 'I can't believe she would come.'

'Lydia Witt? The woman Mom told off?'

Marilyn Beth detached herself to greet the two women. Angelica had been in her class.

'Should we take some Valium?' asked Simon. 'In Mom's honor?' The girl in the wheelchair leaned up to hug Marilyn Beth. 'I thought Angelica Witt was paralyzed from the neck down. She's beautiful!'

Lydia Witt was a carefully preserved matron. Simon recalled a younger Lydia Witt bending over the milk container at Assumption. 'Now I remember her,' he said. 'Mrs Witt.'

The Witts talked with serious faces. Then Marilyn Beth said something. The girl in the wheelchair laughed beautifully. Lydia Witt adjusted her Hermes scarf.

'We better say hello,' said Holly.

Lydia Witt explained she had moved from town years before. While visiting Angelica they had seen the notice in the local paper. 'I always admired your mother,' she said. 'So much.'

'She often talked about you,' Holly said.

Simon felt a tap on his shoulder. Mary Hanson stood behind him in a shabby gray dress.

'I'm so sorry about Mom. She was very beautiful. Why's the casket closed?'

Holly and Marilyn Beth formed a circle around her. 'Mrs Hanson, we were glad you came over the other night,' said Holly. 'We really were.'

Mary Hanson became uncomfortable, unused to fond attention. 'I was in the neighborhood,' she said. 'I saw the lights. Dad was always such a sport. Great guy. Pillar of the democrats. Don't know what we'll do without him.'

There were relatives and democrats and people that no one recognized. Marilyn Beth introduced girls from her office. Simon said, 'Look. It's the hospice nurse. The needle queen.' Soon the man with the blonde curls was at the door frowning. The crowd had thinned. In the hallway, Gerta gave the McNellises long, teary hugs. Vera Sherman arranged for the flowers to be relocated to the church the following morning. The cold air outside was a relief to everyone. May and Adrian drove away, followed by Vera. The children went to Trip's for a drink. They were surprised to find Angelica Witt drinking and talking animatedly in the corner. A friend sat lightly on the arm of her wheelchair.

'I thought she was paralyzed from the neck down,' said Simon. 'She came out better than Peter Gillespie. He was in my class.'

'He was paralyzed from the neck up,' said Marilyn Beth. 'Before the accident.'

When Simon returned to the house on the hill May and Adrian were watching the news. Adrian flicked off the television. They took places around the dining-room table. May held a mug of coffee with white hands. Simon had a fresh beer. Adrian looked for wine. 'I left some here last time. I'm sure June didn't drink all of it. I mean, she was a sick woman.'

'It's on the door,' Simon said.

They talked about Holly and Kevin. Simon said they might not take the house because of financial difficulties.

'I think we should make a big effort to keep the house,' said Adrian. 'We really don't want some stranger here. I'd be willing to help.'

'Oh I agree darlin! It's a wonderful house.'

They talked about current house prices. Simon related Holly's suggestion that he buy the house with her.

'You ought to consider it, tax benefits or not. I think that's what June would have wanted.'

Simon went to the kitchen for another beer. 'It's more complicated than that,' he said. 'Emotionally.' He lit a cigarette.

'I've never seen you smoke, darlin.'

'Sometimes.'

Simon told them of June's earlier plan to give Holly and Kevin the house. 'We fought about it. In India. It was a whopper of a fight.' He gave a brief description. 'It came down to a question of fairness. I was on the right side and she knew it. But it was right after Daddy died.' May offered him another cigarette. He lit it.

'I didn't know any of this,' Adrian said.

'Oh darlin, Mum and I talked about this!' May became excited. 'We talked about it right here at this table! She told me she had been very unfair to you. Very *very* unfair. And she regretted it, darlin. She said you had been right!'

May sat at the table, her dark eyes glowing brightly. Simon looked at the small, eager woman and realized, for the first time, that May *had* gotten into the McNellises. She had been accepted for years. She was, as Adrian liked to point out, *family*. She had learned things. Had June told May about the argument in India? Sitting, as always, at the family table? It was entirely plausible. After death, second hand, through the family, through May – is that how Simon would receive his mother's apology? But it was equally possible that May was lying or half-lying. Had Mom alluded to her sex life to another family widow? Or did May merely wing it with the psychological genius of the born liar? The drapes were drawn, the chandelier glowed in its time-honored way. Simon was home, at the center of his universe, and things were unusually confusing. The trees through Don's greenhouse were impotently still.

'These things get complicated.' Adrian rose, putting a hand on his lower back. 'We've got a big day ahead of us. Did you see my talk?' He pushed toward Simon a sheaf of papers.

'I'll look at it in the morning. And I'll get the lights.'

'Good night darlin!'

Simon McNellis wasn't ready for sleep. He wandered the ground floor. He sat on his mother's bed, comforted by the room's neatness. He went back to the kitchen, switched on the radio and opened a beer. He returned to June's bedroom and opened the tiny drawer of her bedside table. He found two packs of Carltons. He brought the cigarettes to the dining-room table. He dialed Grace's number.

'I'm sorry, I know it's late.' He listened. 'Yes, at ten. Come home afterwards with us. I'll drive you to the station.' He talked a little longer and hung up. He smoked a cigarette, went to the den and returned with his address book. He punched a series of buttons on the cordless telephone and then put it down. He picked it up and called India. But Priscilla couldn't speak for long: she was at the High Commission. He rose, checked the blinking panel at the door and returned to the telephone. He lit another cigarette and opened another beer. He pressed flat the address book and dialed the number in Tokyo he hadn't dialed in ten years. He heard the usual celestial noises and felt a spasm in his bowel. He almost hung up. Then he heard a familiar ring, which brought tears to his eyes.

'Nori? Nori? It's me. Simon. Yes!'

There was an annoying echo on the line. Simon's voice came back to him high and silly. Nori's English faltered.

'I'm in New York. Yes. Yes. Well, no, not exactly. My mother died. She died yesterday.'

May stood in her nightclothes, hand at her chin, staring at the stupid blinkings of the security system. She felt like screaming. She inched forward and peered around the hallway corner. Simon looked like a teenager sitting at the dining-room table in his shirtsleeves. He lit a cigarette and spoke into the telephone. May dashed down the hall, up the stairs and eased her bedroom door shut. She lit a cigarette. First things first, she decided. There was no damn point beginning in the attic, which she knew backward and forward, just because Simon had embarked on a mad, expensive telephone orgy. May had all night. Sleep was a McNellis fetish, unshared and despised by May. There was only one place to start and that was June's bedroom. For May, this night had special meaning. It was the big night, the final night, the star had exploded and May felt at home in the resulting chaos. She prepared to claim from the McNellises what they had steadfastly refused to give – to scoop it up in her widespread arms. On the wall she saw Simon's Christmas present to June. She whispered the words with sarcasm. *May we be unvanquished for a hundred autumns.* She wanted to laugh. It was typical: only the McNellises had to be taught vanquishment by cancer, all the while thinking they had learned something new. Although cancer was nothing to joke over. She stubbed out her cigarette.

150

May had tried her best. She'd given the McNellises much but no one, with the possible exception of Adrian, had cared beyond the courtesies, especially about the damn hotel. She had been forced to find her own account-ant and everyone knew what happened with him. June's illness had clinched it. It all came clear as mountain water: she remained a stranger in the house on the hill. She had been so at Thanksgiving, during the Christmas visit and at the airport as she stood stupidly waiting for a warm car to pull up. Who could blame her for going in for a short cup of hot chocolate? She had given her best to Babe but time proved too short. She opened the door to the attic, moved to the section behind Adrian's room and listened. She heard snoring exactly like Babe's. Tears came to her eyes. She blinked them back. She returned to her room and quietly opened the bedroom door. The down-stairs was dark. She descended the stairs. Simon had gone to bed in the den. May didn't fear discovery this night. Both Adrian and Simon had drunk deeply and grief would provide the ultimate sedation. May ignored the house starts, the furnace screams and the wind outside. She was alone, invincible, in the house June McNellis had tried to control for all time, but which, in the end, vanquished her. May wore Simon's plaid bathrobe, which she had found in the attic closet. She went to June's room and shut the door behind her. She took a cigarette from the bathrobe pocket and stared at June's dresser. May had never dared to disrupt those drawers before. A woman knows nothing more intimately than her drawers, and, in particular, her jewelry drawer. It was an iron-clad inti-macy that nothing disturbed but death. May opened the top drawer. Her eyes widened at the glint of silver. She tapped her cigarette. 'This must be Ruthie's,' she thought, turning the bracelet to look for an inscription. 'She'll be glad to get it back. I'll say: "Ruthie, darlin, June wanted you to have this! It was one of her last wishes. From her very deathbed, darlin." '

It was a long night for May. She stole frequent glances at the window to ensure that dawn was still distant. In the attic closet, behind Simon's room, she pushed aside a rack of clothing and saw the rear of a set of inset drawers. She recalled Daniel's hiding-place and the marijuana she had once discovered there. She knelt down and pushed the bottom drawer forward. She did it slowly: the drawer protruded into the room where Adrian slept. It was possible for sound and even light to glimmer through. She stood and extinguished the overhead light. She found her way back and knelt. Her hand scrabbled in the cement beneath the drawer. She withdrew an old pint bottle. She reached again and felt paper. She withdrew an envelope and then another. In her room, she recognized June's handwriting on an airmail envelope. The second was an envelope with Japanese stamps. She lit a cigarette, opened both letters and read them. May sat with the letters on her lap. She put them in the pocket of her suitcase. Much later, in June's bedroom, she came across a blue envelope in the bottom drawer. It bore writing in June's firm hand. 'Property of June McNellis. To Be Opened After My Death.' She carried it to her room, unopened, and placed it with the other two letters in her suitcase pocket.

She lay in bed, excited and satisfied. Finally, she had penetrated the McNellises. She held one of their secrets – June and Simon McNellis's deepest secret. And, possibly, June McNellis's last thoughts, stuffed in the blue envelope May had been too frightened to violate. She had wanted to slice it open with a fingernail. She'd considered heating the tea kettle for steam. But, in truth, May was intimidated by the words on the envelope written in a dead woman's hand: 'Property of June McNellis.' Once opened, the envelope could not be snuck back in the dresser drawer.

And May was a woman who liked her exits clear, in several directions whenever possible.

Both Adrian and Simon were giving eulogies at June McNellis's funeral. Simon vetted Adrian's at breakfast.

'Yours, Sime?'

'I don't want to show it in advance. It's hard enough as it is.'

'Who's havin my special cinnamon coffee?' May bit into a flaky muffin, catching crumbs with a nervous hand. 'There's one muffin left Adrian darlin. And they're real good.'

The cold had broken. Snow was melting on the street as they drove to the gray church. Vera Sherman was standing on the steps in a fur-collared coat. She squeezed Simon's hand. 'Ready?'

'I guess.'

The family entered behind the casket. The church seemed bigger to Simon and much brighter. Friends and relations craned to look at the family but hastily lowered their gazes before eye-contact was made. The exceptions were Barbara and Grace, who sat beside each other. Barbara gave Simon a blinking, tear-filled smile. Grace nodded seriously and made a quick hand-gesture at the back of her neck. Simon felt his coat collar: it was up. Grace nodded with satisfaction and redirected her gaze to the altar. The family assembled in the front pews. During the first part of the service, the two altar-boys giggled and pointed.

'We did that when I was an altar-boy.' Simon whispered to Holly. 'We always cracked up.'

She replied, 'They're in Jeremy's class.' Jeremy, in a small navy jacket, was flushed.

Adrian's eulogy reminisced about a shared childhood in Brooklyn: lunches at Schraffts, shopping at Dougle's Day-Old Bakery. When Simon ascended to the dais he was startled by the size of the crowd. The church was filled.

'Good morning.' He twisted the microphone downward. 'I am Simon McNellis.' The crowd looked with terrible expectancy. He began. His voice, as it echoed back to him, sounded high and hollow.

'I was always conscious of having a beautiful mother. My sisters felt likewise.' Simon cleared his throat. He tried not to speak too fast. 'We wondered about our friends whose mothers were not beautiful.' There was a stirring in the pews. Someone nervously laughed.

'Later,' Simon said, 'we knew that every mother must be beautiful to the child. But still, there was a difference. We knew it. All we had to do was look at Mom.'

Mary Hanson sat in the front row of Our Lady's chapel. She wore a brown coat lined with worn yellow piling. As an altar-boy, Simon had seen her every morning in the same pew wearing, it seemed, the same ugly coat. She stared at him through thick, greasy glasses. Simon thought of June McNellis's final night: the plump, empty hospital bed, the filmy garbage bags filled with catheters and plastic bedpans, the lush vines on the walls twisting into the shadowed corners. He recalled June's conversation with Mary: her last. And he was inspired by his mother's indomitable decency and her extraordinary will. Simon's nervousness dissolved and his voice strengthened. He came to his conclusion, which was taken from David Copperfield.

' "Can I say of her face – altered as I have reason to remember it, perished as I know it is – that it is gone, when here it comes before me at this instant, as distinct as any face I may choose to look on in a crowded street?" '
He stared at his mother's mourners and felt his predominance. Grace, with eyes wide behind her large glasses, nodded approvingly from a distant pew. Mary Hanson bowed her head. He slowed the words to a crawl. ' "Can I say of her innocent and girlish beauty that it faded and was no more, when its breath falls on my cheek now? Can I say she ever changed, when my remembrance brings her back to life, thus only; and truer to its loving youth than I have been, or man ever is?" '

The family trailed the casket out of church into the warm morning. Grace joined them, hugging Simon slowly and wiping a tear from her cheek. On the steps, a young woman in a black coat rushed to Adrian. 'I loved your speech,' she said. 'My father used to talk about Dougle's Day-Old Bakery!'

Grace sighed and looked down at the ground in disdain. She grabbed Simon's arm tightly and they walked to the car. 'Oh dear,' she said. 'Death does bring out the worst in people.'

From the McNellis driveway, through the greenhouse, party movements could be seen within the house on the hill. Fred McNellis was pouring himself a large drink. Barbara held forth beneath the ferns. She cried, 'Silly Putty!' Vera pushed through the red front door with platters of sandwiches from Jerry's Deli. Aunt Caroline approached Simon in the dining-room with a tight-lipped smile. 'It was beautiful.' She hugged him. 'June would have been proud of you. Proud of you all.' Peter came over, scowling, followed by Susan. He argued with his mother over the Middle East. Caroline's response was a loud, dismissing laugh.

Adrian spent several minutes speaking with a bald man

in a suit. In the kitchen, Simon said, 'Don't you know who that was?'

'I didn't catch his name. He's very fond of June and Don. A local democrat.'

'That's Judge Houlihan.'

Adrian's eyes widened. 'Break out the champagne! My God, have we gone through all of that champagne? This is a scandal: the republicans are sure to make an issue of it.'

The beautiful day dimmed through the beeches. May appeared in a new outfit, ready for the trip into the city with Peter and Susan. She was spending the night. 'I shall return!' she cried. 'Darlins!' Rhonda guided Fred to the door. She whispered to Simon and he felt her nose brush the inside of his ear: 'Don't worry! I'm driving.' Caroline volunteered to drop Adrian at his party in the city. 'Might as well save the train fare,' Adrian said. 'Have you seen my hat, Sime?' Grace joined them. She kissed Simon at the front door.

'When are you planning to go back? I know it's hard.'

'I'll let you know,' said Simon. 'I guess we have a lot of cleaning out to do.'

'Don't throw it all away. I can't tell you the things we lost when my father died. Mother and Cat were *so* ridiculous.'

Finally, it was the McNellises at their places at the table.

'I think that went well.' Simon opened another beer.

'I agree,' said Holly.

'No Winston Rubenoff,' said Marilyn Beth. 'Thank God.'

'I really thought Mimi Spellman would show,' said Holly. 'Mom would have liked that.'

'She did send flowers,' said Simon.

From his nap, Simon awoke to an empty house. He pulled shut the living-room curtains and drew the dining-room drapes. He changed his mind. He preferred the dark backyard with the rumble of the cars speeding away on the invisible thruway. He sat at the dining-room table and looked around the living-room. His eyes met his own. He walked to the coffee table and turned his photo away. He turned on the kitchen television, which showed a fat woman wagging a finger at dormitory schoolgirls: one dark-haired, one blonde, one black. It was his mother's sitcom. He turned it off. The jazz from the radio comforted, but also slowed the passing of time. At home, in India, Simon would have retreated to his computer. But the McNellis house didn't have one. He decided to write thank-yous to June's friends. The only stationery he could find was June's small blue notepaper and envelopes. Dinner was Jerry's sandwiches from the refrigerator. The jazz from the radio provided variable company: sometimes meek and unobtrusive, then poking into all possible corners. The furnace roared and Simon wrote himself a note: 'Furnace – check.'

He called Holly. 'It's lonely over here.'

'Oh, do you want to come for dinner?'

'I've finished. It's okay. For the first time, I can really feel Mom's absence.'

Holly told him to close the windows in case it rained. He called India and said, 'Yeah. I'm all right.' Priscilla described power outages in New Delhi. The line was cut and he chose not to call back. He slept early. A nightmare woke him, set in his mother's bedroom. He was covered in sweat. No one had thought to turn down the furnace with the rise in temperature. Simon noticed an unfamiliar sound. The rain had come. He walked through the ground floor looking for open windows. He adjusted the thermostat; the furnace screams immediately died. Naked, he climbed the stairs and checked his old room, which Adrian was occupying. The windows were closed; Adrian had yet to return from the city. In the girls' room, May's room, he found an open window and closed it. He returned to the den and pulled open a window for air. A horrible cry filled the McNellis house. Simon swung around. He covered his groin. The cry continued: it was a siren. He frantically closed the window he had opened. But the siren continued unpropitiated.

'Holy God.' He spoke aloud. 'The security system.'

Under the siren he heard the ring of the telephone. He ran to his mother's abandoned room and snatched it up. A lazy voice said, 'This is the security agency.'

'I made a mistake. I opened a window. I can't get the siren off.'

'Punch the code,' said the voice.

Simon went to the front door and punched the code into the frantically blinking pad. Nothing happened. He pressed a button marked 'Reset' and entered the numbers again, slowly. 1–9–3–1. But nothing happened. He returned to the phone. The connection was dead.

'They'll hear it in town,' Simon thought. Then he remembered May's open window. He raced to the den, pulled on underpants and climbed the stairs. He slowly reopened May's window. But the siren continued. He stood in the middle of May's room, hands shaking. May's

159

suitcase lay on the bed by the window. It was closed. On top of it lay two rolls of wrapping-paper. One was purple, the other pink.

Simon gingerly lifted the wrapping-paper. He opened the suitcase. Inside, he saw one of his mother's wallets with a paper price tag dangling. He pushed aside a black garment. There was a tape recorder: one of Don's tape recorders from Hong Kong.

The phone rang again. He ran down to his mother's bedroom. He said, 'I pressed the code. It didn't work.'

The bored voice said: 'You have to use the override code.'

'The what?'

'The override code. The emergency code.'

'I don't know the override code! I don't live here! I'm just visiting!' Simon felt like a thief. 'Don't call the police!' And the line cut again.

Simon returned to his room and pulled on pants. The siren blared. The phone rang. He heard Holly's voice but couldn't understand her words.

'I don't know the override code!'

She yelled, 'It's D.O.C.'

Simon ran to the panel, punched the letters and the siren ceased abruptly. The house became dizzyingly still, as if halted after rapid revolutions. He walked to the kitchen and opened a beer. The silence reverberated in his ears. He returned to the front door and disarmed the security system. He waited for Holly to call back. But the phone remained silent.

He returned to May's room. The suitcase was open. He saw a gray cardboard box with a faded pattern of gold leaves. He lifted the top. Inside was a jumble of silver jewelry from June's drawer. He replaced the lid, covered the tape recorder, shut the suitcase and restored the rolls of wrapping-paper. He descended the stairs and locked himself in the den. He removed his pants and underwear and turned off the light. In bed, he tried to defeat the anxiety remaining from the siren. Just when his heart began to calm, the phone rang. He jumped up, naked, and ran to his mother's room.

'I heard the siren.' It was Vera Sherman. 'Are you all right?' He explained and returned to bed. When Simon had achieved a half sleep he heard the sound of the front door opening: Adrian returned from his party in the city. Simon was too drowsy to greet him. But he treasured the sound: the house was no longer empty.

When he awoke the next morning, Holly and Adrian were in the kitchen. Holly said, 'Rough night?' Simon described for Adrian the trauma with the security system.

'Your mother was nutty about that security system.' Adrian rooted through the pantry. 'I'm looking for those lemon preserves. I think we ought to get some enjoyment from them.'

'They're behind the corned-beef hash,' said Simon. 'I kind of hid them from May.' But no one could find the lemon preserves.

Holly held a paper packet of coffee. 'I hate cinnamon coffee.'

'Come here everyone,' said Simon. 'I have something to tell you.' He described his discovery of the previous night.

Holly stood up. 'I'm searching that bitch's bags.'

They climbed the stairs to the girls' room. Adrian said, 'I don't know if this is *right*.' His voice dropped to a whisper as they entered the bedroom. 'What if she walks *in*?'

'I knew she bought these for herself.' Holly threw the wrapping-paper on the floor. 'They're Easter colors.'

'I don't know if we should actually go so far as to open someone's bag,' said Adrian.

'Stop me,' muttered Holly. She unabashedly rearranged May's clothes, producing item after item. 'Look.'

'It's Mom's wallet,' explained Simon. 'We saw it in her

161

drawer. The day she died. Mom had two. May has taken one.' Holly threw the tape recorder on the bed, followed by a pair of cuticle scissors. Simon picked them up. '*I* wanted these.'

'The jewelry's junk, thank God.' Holly produced *Decorating Rich* from the bottom of the suitcase. She wagged it at Adrian and Simon. 'She's gone through every room in this entire house. From the basement to the attic. That bitch! I'm so goddamned mad!'

'How did she get this?' Simon looked at the big book. 'It was in the den. In the back of the closet.'

'Adrian?' Holly flushed with triumph. She passed along the lemon preserves.

'Extraordinary,' said Adrian. 'I don't think anyone should stoop so low as to steal people's preserves.'

'Here's the other coffee. She left us with the cinnamon shit.' Holly opened May's second suitcase and withdrew a large parcel. She threw it to Simon. It was three rolls of toilet-paper in a wrapper with a baby on the front.

'I bought these,' said Simon.

Then came a pair of silver candlesticks, a silver-framed photo of June McNellis as a girl and a rusting pressure-cooker. Holly gave a cry. 'Look at this!' She unwrapped a tea cup from a silk shirt. A matching saucer followed. 'It's Mom's pattern! The bitch was stealing Mom's china! I knew it all along. But Mom's pattern!' She held up the cup, bone colored with gold edges.

'What's that?' Simon withdrew from the suitcase an orange plastic vial. He read the label. 'It's Mom's pain-killer. I threw these away the night Mom died. May went through the garbage. As soon as she arrived.'

'She stole drugs?' Adrian asked.

'Narcotics,' said Holly. 'We could call the cops.'

Downstairs, Adrian paced the living-room, peering through the front windows. His voice kept dropping to a guilty hush, as if May was an invisible element of the

162

atmosphere. 'She's part of the family, after all. I don't think it behooves any of us . . . '

'What about our stuff?' said Holly. 'May is stealing our heirlooms. Your sister's things.'

Adrian winced and pushed his hand at the air between himself and Holly. 'Stop it, stop it! We'll get it all back. *I'll* get it back if I have to. But let May get out of the house tomorrow morning. Let's get this whole funeral thing behind us. Afterwards I'll take care of it. There's no point in having the whole family fighting. After all, Holly, no one's perfect.'

'That's not the point, Adrian.'

'You're not perfect either, Simon.'

'I didn't say I was perfect!'

Adrian's view prevailed. May was to be given safe passage the following morning. Adrian vowed to retrieve the stolen goods and he pointed out that the thefts couldn't be considered grand larceny.

'She's broken up Mom's china set,' protested Holly. 'I consider that a hostile act. She might as well have stamped on that cup and saucer. That woman's sick.'

They returned to the dining-room. They concurred that Marilyn Beth should be kept in the dark. Holly disappeared and came back with the bottom of a brass egg. She thrust it at Adrian.

'I found this on Mom's dresser. Look.' The egg was dirty with four cigarette butts. 'She sat smoking as she went through Mom's drawers.'

Adrian and Simon examined the cigarette butts. 'They're her brand,' said Simon. Adrian shook his head.

It was important for Adrian to get the solemn agreement of Holly and Simon. For Kevin was about to pick him up for the airport. In another couple of hours, May would return from the city to the McNellis house and remain there until her plane departed the following morning.

Holly departed with a final shot at Adrian: 'I don't

163

think Mom would have handled it this way.' Her Volvo shot away and pulled into Vera Sherman's driveway.

'She's upset,' Adrian said. 'And I don't blame her. But we've got to stick together on this.'

An hour later, Adrian gave Simon a gentlemanly hug on the doorstep. 'For peace in the family, almost anything is worth it.' He straightened his Irish hat. Simon nodded. Shortly after Adrian left Holly called.

'I'm at Vera's,' she said. 'I've told her everything. I still think I might say something. Before May leaves.'

On Saturday evening, Vera Sherman watched the McNellis house from her kitchen window. A taxi pulled up the driveway and Vera telephoned Holly. 'She's back. I think they're in the kitchen. I'll keep an eye.' Later Vera saw Simon's car drive toward town. The greenhouse went blue with television light. Then it darkened. The light in the girls' room went on and stayed on. Shortly afterward, the yellow rectangles appeared on the beeches at the far side of the McNellis house. Vera picked up the telephone. 'She's in your mother's room.' The voice on the other end cursed. 'No, I don't think there's anything we can do.' The rectangles suddenly vanished. Vera recalled those happy views of the past: the cars parked violently on the summer lawn, the house ablaze with lights the night Marilyn Beth was born. How excited Ross had been – how he had stammered when he called the hospital. The McNellis house was Vera Sherman's second home, especially since Ross's death. The view from her kitchen window was a family photo. But the house on the hill was transforming. This night, it seemed cold and alien, a house in which every new light winked malignly through her kitchen curtains. Worse: an unpopulated ruin with scavengers. In the past it had spoken in soft cries of children. Now it was silent. And when it did call to her, as it had the previous evening, waking her from a weak sleep, it screamed. Vera had listened to the siren and watched the frantic lights flash on and off throughout the house. Her hand was on the telephone – but she no longer knew whether to call. The siren blared. And then it had ceased. She had returned to bed, feeling a blackness between the houses. She finally called from the bedroom, relieved at Simon's frightened voice. They all felt the same. June McNellis was dead and the vacuum was screaming.

After midnight, May heard the downstairs door slam. Simon had returned. She waited as long as she could and then peered from the top of the stairs into perfect darkness.

'If these McNellises stopped drinking,' she thought, 'half their problems would be solved.' She stubbed out her cigarette. 'They'd live a sight longer too.'

May had quitted Peter and Susan as rapidly as was politely possible, pleading grieving relatives in the suburbs. Peter refused one of May's choicest finds from June's dresser: Babe's diary from high school. She held it in her hand: a gray, hardbound diary written in a beautiful Catholic schoolboy script. Peter had said, 'That's the last thing I want in my life.' Susan had nodded solemn agreement. May said, 'But look, darlin! Look at all these wonderful descriptions of your father's life when he was just a boy – like old snapshots!' She opened a page. It contained, like so many damn pages, a description of Babe's sister's active social life in wartime Brooklyn. June McNellis had blinded them all. They should all be glad she was gone: the goddess proved mortal, the blazing sun exposed as a pitiful twinkle magnified by some cheap, carnival stage mirror.

May was fully packed and had only two pieces of unfinished business. She had decided to return June's dying missive to her family. The risk was too high: the children might have been alerted – a typical June ploy – and May had yet to perfect the steaming open of envelopes. At the same time, she had a steady grasp of what could be removed from a house without notice: spare wallets, uncounted cups, anything that was stocked in bulk or had an inch of basement dust on it. This included, May calculated, old letters hidden behind drawers. It never ceased to amaze May how foggy people were about the goods in their own houses.

May regretted her haste on the evening of June's wake. She had struck gold but she had been hasty. What else remained? She removed the three letters from her purse, including June's sealed blue envelope, and tucked them into the pocket of the plaid bathrobe. She opened the small door to the attic closet and moved down its length. She pushed aside clothing. She switched on the dim over-head light and knelt at the drawers extending from Simon's old room, now unoccupied. She pushed the top drawer halfway. She pushed the middle drawer the same distance. She pushed the bottom drawer all the way to expose scrabbled cement floor. She thought of Daniel's marijuana, discovered in the same way so many years before. How important it had seemed! How trivial compared to the secrets May had uncovered in the dirt of the McNellis attic – giving her the intimate entrée she had craved for a decade.

Simon McNellis stood in the dark behind the closed door of his boyhood bedroom. He had drunk a lot of beer and was beginning to regret his secret watch. May's door hadn't even opened; her rampage had obviously ended. Simon's eyelids were falling and he was thinking, 'Let her keep the damn toilet-paper.' A sound came from the opposite end of the room. He dismissed it as a stray house noise. Then a crack of light appeared from the far wall.

168

It grew into a thin rectangle and then a thicker one. Finally, dim light streamed into the room, illuminating him behind the door.

'She's in the attic.' He walked to the small louvered door and lifted the latch soundlessly. He opened the door, ducked his head and stepped inside.

The attic was lit but empty. Simon started to retreat when he saw two small feet protruding from a row of clothes. He moved forward. May was on her knees, tiny and doll-like, rummaging fiercely.

'May?'

She straightened up. 'Oh, darlin!' She stood abruptly, holding her hands before her as if they were dirty. 'I was just . . . why I was just . . . ' She laughed and wiped her hands on the robe. 'Darlin, I was just lookin for a suitcase. I've run out of room! I guess I just shopped too damn much.' She smiled sweetly. 'As usual.'

'You're wearing my robe?' Simon saw the drawers pushed inward.

'I'm sorry darlin. Did you need it? I thought it was one of the girls'.'

'What are you doing behind those drawers?'

'What drawers, darlin?'

His anger welled. 'You're caught, May.'

'Whatever do you mean darlin?' May spoke with girlish innocence.

'You've been stealing. We've caught you.'

'Why darlin.' She pushed the clothes back into place.

'We went through your suitcases this morning. We found all that stuff.'

May stared blankly. One of her hands traced a line on her chin.

'We found the china. And Mom's wallet.'

'No, darlin.'

'Yes May.'

'Who is we?'

'Holly and me. And Adrian.'

'Well darlin, Adrian didn't say a *thing* to me. I talked to him on the phone just this evenin.'

'You're caught, May. You've been stealing from a dead woman. From our dead mother.'

'Darlin, there must be some terrible misunderstanding. Your mother gave me that wallet.'

'What?'

'Yes, darlin. We bought it together. At Odd Lots. And she said, at Christmas . . . '

Simon was confused. 'What about the china?'

'What china?'

'Mom's setting.'

'Oh darlin. Are you talking about that cup and saucer? Didn't Mum tell you I was buying her china? Haven't I told you about this *wonderful* shop with discontinued patterns? Every time I come up I bring another place setting . . . '

Simon shook his head. 'May. We've got you. We found the drugs in your suitcase. We found the toilet-paper.'

May looked at him sadly. 'Toilet-paper darlin?'

'I'm going downstairs. I'm calling Holly.'

'Wait!' said May. 'Don't! This is all gettin so ugly.'

'Forget it May.'

'I said don't!' May's eyes were wide and scared. She pulled two airmail envelopes from the pocket of the robe. 'Don't you dare bring anybody else into it. This is between just you and me, darlin.' She waved the envelopes. 'I've read these. I know all about you and Nori.' She spoke the foreign name with a sneer. 'And, of course, our dear, deceased, darlin June.'

Simon looked at the rack of clothes. He walked to it and separated the old coats. The drawers were pushed forward. 'That's what you were doing. Give me those letters.'

May shrunk back onto the boxes at the rear of the attic.

'Give me!'

'Have them.' She threw the letters. Two thin envelopes, askew on the plank floor, with ragged edges and canceled stamps. 'I don't need them. I know them by heart.'

'What do you know?'

May straightened herself, fixed the robe and combed her hair with one hand. 'I know, darlin, you knocked the poor girl up. I know she had an abortion. And I know your dear mother refused to have anything to do with her. And with *you* if you married her. Because the McNellises "can't accept such a thing – ever." '

The quote from the letter transported Simon ten years and thousands of miles. He was in the room again, a tiny Japanese room with a dim overhead light, reading the short, angry letter that had directed his life like a boulder pushed into a virgin stream. He was on that claustrophobic Tokyo lane, walking away from the unyielding, teary mother in the fur coat, looking back once – or so it was supposed to be. And he was at the crowded airport, ticket in hand, baggage to be worried about, saying goodbye to the Japanese woman who had aborted his baby. Who had done nothing wrong but loved him. She walked away hurriedly in a dress he'd never forgotten, with crimson blossoms along the hem. She tripped slightly and shook her head. She didn't look back, although Simon had watched and waited.

'Mom was wrong!' Simon cried.

'You obeyed her,' said May triumphantly. 'Because the McNellises would never accept such a thing – *ever*!'

Simon looked around the narrow attic with its artifacts from his childhood. 'I believed her.'

'I read your letter too,' May said. 'Why didn't you go through with it?'

'I don't know.'

'You were a damn fool.' May straightened up from the boxes. 'And now, I'm the only one who knows. June is dead. The secret was almost buried. But *I* know! I'll tell your sisters.'

Simon revived from the shock of May's discovery. He watched her leer at him from the rear of the dim attic. Her hands moved before her restlessly.

'Tell them.' Simon moved to the small door.

'You didn't even pay for the poor girl's abortion!'

'Shut up!'

'You're weak!' cried May. 'Like the whole damn McNellis family! Except June!'

'We'll see,' said Simon. 'I'm calling Holly. Maybe we'll call the police.'

'Wait! That's not all!'

'May, stop this bullshit!'

'Look!' May withdrew the blue envelope. Simon could read the letters printed in his mother's unmistakable hand: 'Property of June McNellis. To Be Opened After My Death.'

'What does it say?'

'It's mine!' said May. 'Don't tell anyone – and you can have it!'

'What does it say?'

'It's to you, darlin!' May returned to her sugary, sympathetic self. 'It's a letter to you! It's your mother's last apology.'

'Give it to me.'

May thrust the blue envelope into her nightgown. 'The letter's hidden. This is just the envelope.'

'What do you want?'

'Keep my secret. And I'll keep yours. Then you can have the letter. I'll mail it to you, darlin. I will.'

Simon hesitated.

'She mentions it darlin. She talks about Nori. And your fight over the house too. But I'll destroy the damn letter. Then none of you will get to read it. If you don't protect me. Cause I didn't do anything wrong, darlin. I just wanted a little share – my share. I just wanted you all to accept me.'

May looked at Simon with terror. Her hand rose from her chest and pointed. He said, 'May?' He turned. Vera Sherman, in a raincoat, stood behind Simon. She extended her hand. 'I've heard it all. Give me the letter May.'

'No!' cried May. She crumpled against the soft brown boxes.

'I saw the lights. I know the security code.' Vera stepped forward and extended her hand. 'Give me the letter or I'll go in there and find it.' May removed the blue envelope from her breast and placed it in Vera's unwavering hand.

Vera turned it over. 'It's unopened. Good for you, May.' She placed the letter in her raincoat pocket. She stooped and picked up the letters on the floor. She handed them to Simon. 'These are family things, May. They're none of your business. Get your bags. You can stay at my house tonight.' She walked calmly out of the attic.

Simon said, 'Leave Mom's stuff on the bed, May.'

Simon carried the bags to the door. They were half-empty. He watched as May and Vera pulled them down the hill and across the street. He went to the kitchen, turned on the lights and opened a beer. But the blackness of the windows repelled him. He extinguished the lights and walked through the living-room, stopping at the pink portrait of June McNellis in her prime. He said, 'Oh, Mom. It never ends.' He went to his mother's room and opened the letters on her bed. He read them, remembering each word. He sat with the letters on his lap and looked around the room. He closed his eyes and tried to summon his mother. But her spirit was no longer there. When his eyes opened, he saw a room with pretty floral wallpaper and a neat, single bed with a delicate headboard. He left the lights on intentionally, but it was an empty gesture. He was alone in the quiet house. For the first time, he didn't bother shutting the den door before he slept.

The next day, Marilyn Beth brought Jerry's sandwiches for lunch. Vera Sherman described May's departure. 'She was very silent. We didn't talk all the way to the station.'

'Did you x-ray her bags?' Marilyn Beth pulled her hair into a thick ponytail. 'I still think we should have called the cops.'

Vera took a blue envelope from her pocket, handed it to Holly and left. Simon said: 'I'm dreading this.'

There were two letters in the envelope. The first was dated October 1989. Simon said: 'Before her trip to India.'

Dear Holly, Simon and Marilyn Beth,
Through the years of going on aeroplanes I have
always had a letter in my drawer. Last year's would
be destroyed and replaced with this year's. I am not
going to destroy the last one, old as it is, because I
want you to have it.
Some additions are necessary. Marilyn, I'm very glad
that I saw you graduate, go to Mexico, find a job
and be on your own. I do not wish to die, but I do
miss Don very much and since this means that we
are together again, it should be consolation to you.
Hopefully I will live to see more grandchildren and
see them grow but if I don't it is up to all of you to

*maintain a close and loving McNellis family as Don
and I tried so very hard to do.*

The letter was signed with a single, ugly 'M.' It had a
postscript:

Don't mourn, it read. *Just remember the laughs.*

The earlier letter was dated 1985. It was addressed to
Don.

*Dear Don,
Perhaps it is foolish to leave this but I feel I must.
First, but most important, I have had a very good
life. God has been more than good to me and I think
he understood my fear of what old age could possibly
bring.
Our marriage has – I think – been a good one. I've
loved you for a very long time. And still do. Trite as
it is to say, the world goes on. I hope you'll be happy
and maybe even happier. However, I repeat, Wife
No. 2 does not get my furniture or any jewelry. The
children know what things I'm referring to.
Holly, Simon and Marilyn Beth: I love you very much
and have always been proud of you. Remain as you
are – McNellises – and all will be perfect. No disputes
about money or anything else.
My love to the little ones.*

This one was signed in two fashions: a confident 'June'
and, beneath it, another scrawled 'M.'

Marilyn Beth went to the kitchen, wiping her face. Holly
said in a low tone, 'I don't like the sound of that second
letter.'

Simon shook his head. 'I agree.' He reread both letters.
'She wanted us to read it.'

Adrian called that evening. He said he had spoken to May
on the telephone.

'Did she come clean?' asked Simon.

'Not exactly,' said Adrian. 'In fact, she went on and on about the wallet. She insists your mother gave it to her.'

'We can reduce the charges by a count.'

'Actually,' Adrian said, 'I think she expected me to take her side. I think she was trying to pull one over on me. But I said to her, "May. I know about the preserves. I don't think anyone should steal a person's lemon preserves." I think that got her. Yup – that really got her.'

On Monday, June's ashes were ready for burial. The ceremony was officiated by the priest with the mustache. Only the McNellis children attended, along with Vera Sherman. At the last moment, Barbara pulled up in her BMW with a large bouquet of flowers. It was a warm winter day. June's ashes were in a small can on a piece of brightly-colored artificial turf. Marilyn Beth whispered, 'Daddy's had a flip-top lid.' Barbara put her hands on her hips and laughed at a ninety-degree angle.

On the way home, Holly and Kevin announced their decision not to take the house. They couldn't afford it.

'And something's different,' said Holly. 'I don't think I want to live there anymore.'

'I don't blame you,' said Simon. 'I don't want to stay there another night.'

'Do you want to move over to our house?'

'No,' said Simon. 'Actually, it's good for me to stay there. To say goodbye.'

The curtains and drapes were removed for the cleaners. Old clothes were collected in garbage bags, which were dumped in the living-room beneath the famous portrait of June McNellis. Simon said, 'Who's taking this?'

'There's no room in my house,' said Holly.

'It's a shame, isn't it?' June McNellis flexed her perfect chin toward the ceiling. Cracks had been exposed by new

176

light coming through the curtainless windows. 'It seemed like such a permanent thing.'

'Maybe Adrian will take it,' said Holly. 'He wants to ship some other things. Like Doc's desk. And the rocker.'

'It's funny: I never thought there'd be a cut-off between the generations. I thought these artifacts would follow us around forever.'

'Not if you have a house my size,' said Holly.

When they were cleaning out the den, Marilyn Beth came across a removable panel in the closet ceiling. Behind it was a recessed space. She called down from the stepladder, 'Uh-oh. We've got some skin up here.' She threw a heavy stack of magazines to the floor.

'They must be mine,' said Simon. 'From high school. How did they get in the closet?' Simon looked through them. 'These are *Hustlers*. I never had *Hustlers*. I've only seen one copy in my life.'

'Look at this, guys. A bag of condoms.'

'*Those* are mine,' said Simon. 'Daddy found them in my bathroom. He gave me a lecture.'

'Daddy gave you a lecture?' asked Holly.

'I was never so embarrassed in my life.' Marilyn Beth was rooting through the bag with a frown.

'The bag is from McCullough's Pharmacy?' asked Simon.

'It's from a pharmacy in El Paso,' she said.

'El Paso?'

'Daddy's business trips,' said Holly.

'Oh God.'

'Throw them *away*.' Marilyn Beth tossed the bag. The condoms, pink and black, spilled on the carpet.

Holly climbed the stepladder to inspect the secret place. 'Mom would never have looked up here. Above the closet.' She descended the ladder. Simon did his inspection.

'What else did she find when he died?'

Simon said, 'We'll never know.'

'Daddy always did have a taste for Tex-Mex,' said Marilyn Beth. ' "Dirty Don." '

Holly shook her head. 'I'm so glad I'm not taking this house.'

During a cleaning break, Marilyn Beth said, 'I was sitting on the toilet this morning. I thought: "I hope Mom can't see me now."'

'I agree,' said Holly. 'For her sake.'

'It was not pretty,' said Marilyn Beth. 'I don't know how you can drink so much beer.'

Simon didn't reply. He thought of himself the previous evening, masturbating with the den door open. He wondered how he looked from above. For Nori had come back to him with an obsession. He imagined her every night, and during the days, with extraordinary intensity. If his mother could see, he decided, it was her own fault.

Simon said, 'I thought you might like this.' He presented Holly with the framed Vedic verse he had given June for Christmas.

'Thank you. I'd love it.'

'I had it made especially,' Simon admitted.

She read from it: '*May we be in our places for a hundred autumns.*'

'Beautiful, isn't it? What else could anyone want?'

Marilyn Beth volunteered to drive Simon to the airport. As the car pulled away, he bid his silent goodbye to the house on the hill as he had so many times before. The exterior was the same: the square stone face with its handsome windows. For a second, he was annoyed by its changelessness. Then he summoned his own portrait of June McNellis standing at the doorway with her ugly cane, wearing Doc's long sweater, waving her cigarette in a brave arc, more beautiful than at any other time. It was an image he treasured because it was his: a farewell his sisters had not received. He had imagined a message: *Break free!* And now there was nothing to break free from. Just an empty suburban house.

The voice from a dream, scarred with illness: *I've had it all! Can't you take it? Can't I pass it on? Are none of you worthy of me? I've had it all! Am I too late?*

Marilyn Beth talked about Mexico. 'There's no point staying around here anymore. That's how I figure it.'

'*Es el hombre . . .*'

'*. . . que tiene las llaves en la mano.*'

'*En el mano.*'

'Who gives a fuck.' She weaved aggressively through traffic. 'I'm hoping the Mexicans are a bit loose with the language.'

Simon hummed involuntarily. Marilyn Beth smiled. 'Does Mama's little baby love shortnin, shortnin? Does he still, the little darlin?'

'No more darlins. I never want to hear that word again.'

Later, he asked, 'Bethy, why didn't you cut your hair before Mom died? You said you were going to. You know how much it would have meant to her.'

'She's dead, Simon.' Marilyn Beth frowned at the rear-view mirror. 'I don't think it's a good idea to live our lives for a dead woman.' She looked at him. 'Any of us.'

At the airport he kissed her goodbye. 'Will you write, Bethy? From Mexico?'

'I'm terrible with letters.'

'I'll write you.'

She zipped her leather jacket against the cold. 'I'll try. I'll really try.'

A movie flickered on the small, airplane screen. Simon looked at the people around him: tourists in hopeful summer cottons, Indians eagerly awaiting the touch of native soil beneath their sandals. He thought of Marilyn Beth's comment – 'There's no point staying around here anymore' – and felt the same about his return to India. All the cables had snapped, even the longest, the most sinuous, the one that had grown most rigid and sacred over the years: the one connecting and separating June and Simon McNellis.

Simon thought of the McNellis house, darkened and abandoned on its small, proud hill. Darkened as the family had never imagined it; empty as it never had been. Or perhaps not quite empty. When the mother's light died, the ghosts had risen from the shadows, dispelled no longer. But new lights would come to the house, expecting, without recognizing it, to shine forever. They'd vanquish the last remaining ghosts of the McNellis era. And create their own shadows and shades.

Simon looked through the window at the Siberian snow. He recalled the horrible unquiet nights as the McNellis house groaned and shrieked, laboring to expel its cold, waxen issue and a disintegrated womb. He recalled May, the wicked midwife, shrunken at the back of the attic, her hands clasped before her.

'Oh Mom. You were lucky to miss it.' He whispered, not in deference to his seatmate, who was plugged into the movie. A whisper had more power. 'But you would have gotten one hell of a story out of it.'

In Delhi the bad dreams began. His mother called; she lived again; she died again. He wrapped himself in the plaid blanket and looked down on the abandoned Indian street, smoking cigarette after cigarette. Simon had held India at a distasteful distance; suddenly he longed for its embrace. All the things the McNellises had disdained – caste, class, religion – held Indians fast and content. What did it mean to transcend class or religion but to lose them? And family: an embrace Simon had spent ten years trying to simultaneously accept and evade. But now it was too late. Simon lit a cigarette and looked at the cracked Indian street, lit by an iron, old-fashioned streetlamp. A turbaned guard strolled languidly. He felt rootless, high on his balcony in the deep, smoky Indian night.

Not rootless. He looked at the opaque sky. Sunless: he had lost his eyelike star!

May we be unvanquished for a hundred autumns . . . May we be in our places . . . May we delight and rejoice . . .

'*May we be hearing and speaking for a hundred autumns,*' Simon whispered. '*May we be able to see this sun for a long time.*' He gave in to his new fantasies: that he would hear his mother's call on a crowded street, turn, find nothing; that she would follow his life, appreciating

181

and disapproving; that she would somehow yank those hard, vital cables. Surely they hadn't gone limp so quickly!

But the fantasies were never realized except in vivid, uncomforting dreams. Even the dreams had a cruel elusiveness: charged with an emotion Simon could never recapture once his eyes were opened.

July–October 1990
New Delhi